BAD TEACHER

CLARISSA WILD

Copyright © 2016 Clarissa Wild
All rights reserved.
ISBN: 978-1534702950
ISBN-10: 1534702954

© 2016 Clarissa Wild

This is a work of fiction. Names, characters, places and incidents are either the product of the author's imagination or are used fictitiously. Any resemblance to actual events, places, organizations, or person, whether living or dead, is entirely coincidental.

All rights reserved. No part of this book may be reproduced, transmitted in any form or by any means, electronic or mechanical, including photocopying, recording, or by any information storage retrieval system. Doing so would break licensing and copyright laws.

Music Playlist

"Did It Again" by Shakira
"Close" by Nick Jonas ft. Tove Lo
"Hands To Myself" by Selena Gomez
"Perfect" by Selena Gomez
"My Love" by Route 94 ft. Jess Glynne
"Style" by Taylor Swift
"Personal Jesus" by Marilyn Manson
"Gibberish" by MAX
"Style" cover by MAX & Nick Dungo
"Wrong" by MAX
"Teen Idle" by Marina And The Diamonds
"Only Human" by Cold Showers
"Into You" by Ariana Grande
"You & I (Forever)" by Jessie Ware
"Habits Of My Heart" by Jaymes Young
"What Is Love" by Jaymes Young
"Red" by Hyuna
"Kitty Hawk" by Ki:Theory

Chapter 1

THOMAS

The music isn't the only thing in this club that's hard.
What, too much?
Deal with it.
There's nothing wrong with wanting to get laid. It's a good way to blow off steam.
Talking about steam ... God, just looking at all these girls glistening with sweat as they shake their asses makes me horny. Time to find what I came here for.
I slide through the people across the dance floor, tapping my foot a few times because the music is so damn catchy. They're playing a good old 90's song called "My Love" by Route 94, and I can feel the bass vibe through my skin. As I check out all the girls around me, I let myself go

with the music, dancing to the beat.

I glance around the room and spot a girl with a drink in her hand, dancing on her own.

And not just any girl.

That girl.

The girl with the smoking hot body, barely hidden in a pink knee-length skirt and crop top, dancing on black leather wedges. Her bob cut hair, all shades of red, sways while she shuffles on her feet, casually sipping from her drink. Her eyes are focused on the floor, like she's not even aware of the fact that she's being watched. And oh … do I love watching her.

After a few seconds, she sits down at the bar, taking a quick sip of her drink, while I sit down at the other end and watch her from the corner of my eye.

She turns her head, and in an instant, our eyes connect.

Smoldering heat.

That's all there is as the people around us dance, but I don't even see them anymore. All I see is her. *That girl* … the girl I'm going to bang tonight.

That's what I came here for.

Is it shallow?

Maybe, but then again … nothing wrong with just wanting a fuck.

And by the looks of it, so does she.

Her eyes glimmer in the dark, a curious smile on her face. A green and purple flash of light reflects from her nose where a tiny crystal bud rests. I can't help but wonder where else she has those.

She sets her empty glass down, gets up, and turns around, but not before throwing a final glance at me. I get up too and follow her through the dancing crowd. She disappears behind a column, and I lose sight of her.

No fucking way she's getting away.

I follow her trail through the club, passing through the crowd like they don't even matter. I've seen many girls come and go, but this one, in particular, catches my eye more than any of the other girls here do. I don't know. All I know is I have to find her.

So I keep looking until I finally do.

There, in the middle of the dance floor alone, she dances. Her fingers brush through her hair as she sways her hips, her eyes closed, focused on the sound of the music drowning out whatever needs to be silenced.

Just the way I like it.

I step closer until she finally raises her head and sees me.

Her eyes, hidden under thick lashes, sparkle with enthusiasm as she looks up at me. She playfully bites her lip as I approach, and I reciprocate with an added tongue swipe.

Her brow rises as I place my hand on her hip, pulling her closer toward me.

She hesitates a second, but when the beat drops, her hands slide up to my shoulders, and she starts to dance. The friction between us is undeniable, her ass swaying side to side against my hands. I cop a feel, which she doesn't seem to mind. We inch closer and closer, her eyes irresistible, but her mouth even more so. When our lips almost touch, her lips part.

"Who are you?" she whispers.

"Call me John …" I murmur.

"John who?"

"John Doe."

She smirks. "Your real name."

I twirl her around in my arm and lean on her shoulder, my lips dangerously close to her neck. She takes in a sharp breath of air as my teeth graze her skin, my breath probably already setting her on fire.

"Do you really want to know?"

Slowly, she nods her head.

"Hmm ... all right. Because you're so curious. Let's do two questions."

"Two?"

"You ask me a question, I answer, then I ask you a question, and you answer."

"Okay. Who goes first?" she asks.

"You." I smirk.

"Why did you pick me?"

"I saw you in your high heels and your tight skirt. I like how you looked back," I whisper, licking my lips. "My turn. Do you like to dance with strangers?"

"Is that a real question?"

"Ah-ah," I say. "Can't answer with a question."

"Okay. Well, then I guess ... maybe?"

"Hmm ..."

Her hips grind against mine as we lose ourselves in the music. My body close to hers, it's almost as if we're becoming one. We don't know each other ... and that makes it perfect.

"My turn," she says. "Do you do this often?"

"Yes."

"That's not really an answer," she says.

"Then don't ask a question that can be answered with just one word," I muse.

She sighs. "You're a know-it-all, aren't you?"

"I just like games and rules," I say with an arrogant smile. "Last one ... What would you say if I took you home tonight and fucked you like you've never been fucked before?"

She sucks in a short breath.

I place a hand over her mouth. "Don't answer yet. Dance with me first."

We dance some more, my hands incapable of staying off her. As I become heady from the lust, I press a soft, succulent kiss on her neck, which creates goose bumps all over her body. Her body melts in my arms, and my cock stiffens in response.

"I can't control myself ..." I whisper into her ear.

She twists around in my arms again, and we dance closer than before, my hands on her body in places they shouldn't be. She leans in, so I go in for the kill.

I kiss her full on the lips, enjoying the spicy taste of her drink.

She kisses me back just as fervently, and I take it as a sign to kiss her harder, faster. I show her what's in store for her if she goes home with me. And right when she becomes needy, I stop, pull back, and let her suck in the empty air.

"Are you game?" I ask.

"Yeah ..." she mutters under a heavy breath.

"No names. No numbers."

"Isn't that dangerous?"

"Fuck yes, it is."

"Hmmm ..." A smile forms on her lips. "I like dangerous."

I grin. "You sure, redhead?"

She grabs my hand firmly, which tells me she's ready.

And it also tells me she's just as nuts as I am.

Going home with a stranger to have sex with them is pretty much the most reckless thing you can do. But it's also one of the most exciting things ever, and I know she knows that too. I can see it in her eyes.

So I pull her with me, away from the crowd, and out of the club.

I hail a cab and open the door for her like a true gent. I slide in after her and tell the cabby to drive us to my place. She sits in the corner, her fingers curling through her hair as she stares out the window. When I clear my throat, she looks my way.

"You know you can say no anytime you want. Turn this cab around. You'd never hear from or see me again."

"I know." She shrugs.

I slide closer and put my arm around her. "Or … I can show you the night of your life."

She grins. "Now, you're talking."

Minutes later, we're stumbling through my apartment door, kissing and tearing our clothes off each other. Her kisses are reckless and wet and so fucking good that I can't get enough of them. She struggles to breathe as my tongue dips into her mouth, and I circle around, wanting more.

I pull her with me through my living room, and when only her bra and panties are left, I shove her up against my wall.

"You ready for this?" I growl.

"Yes …"

"You sure 'bout that? Things can get … rough."

"I like rough," she hums, biting her lip again.

Goddammit, it's so fucking hot; I want to ravish her.

So I press a kiss to her neck and suck, hard—so hard it leaves a red mark, and a short moan escapes her mouth.

"I'll hear more of those tonight ..." I murmur against her ear, as I take her earlobe into my mouth and suck.

"Give it to me," she whispers.

I nibble a little. "Oh, I can give it to you all right ... but it's gonna be my way only."

I cup her tit and squeeze, moaning as I take her mouth with mine. I can't help it; I'm always a little possessive over the girls I conquer, but this one especially.

I don't know why, but there's something about her ... something mysterious that I want to discover.

"You have courage," I whisper against her lips. "Going along with a stranger, having wild sex."

"I'm just very naïve ..." she muses playfully. "Or I just know who to trust."

"Do you now?" I raise a brow. "Well, you picked the wrong guy."

"Good. I like wrong."

Her grin makes me want to grab her and show her who's in charge.

But ... I don't want to push it ... yet.

First, she needs to relax. Maybe a good pussy tonguing will do. Then comes the hard fuck.

I lick her lips as I pull her bra off in one go, which seems to surprise her a little.

"Had practice," I say.

"I can tell."

"Is that wrong?"

"I know I'm not the first ..." She shrugs. "I like a man

who knows what he's doing."

"Good, because I sure as fuck do." I kiss her and then lower myself until I'm right in front of her panties. I hook my fingers under the fabric and pull it down her legs.

Her pussy glistens with wetness as I slide a finger up and down her slit. She shudders with delight.

"How long has it been?" I ask. "You seem ... nervous."

"Not gonna tell," she says.

"Hmm ... You know I'll want to make you tell me."

She licks her bottom lip, seductively gazing down at me. "Try me."

Oh ... I will.

I give her a wicked smile and then lean in, blowing hot air onto her eager pussy. Goose bumps scatter, and I take it as a sign to dive in. Her moans entice me as I lick her pussy, swiveling my tongue back and forth across her slit. She tastes so fucking good; I could do this all night long.

My cock grows, tenting my pants as I suck her wet pussy dry. I fucking love the taste of her, and it makes me want to put my hands all over her. But first, she has to come.

I circle her clit and press down, making her squeal with delight, her fingers scratching my back.

"Fuck ..." she moans.

"I will soon, but I want you to come first."

"Like this? I don't know if I can ..."

"Sure you can." I grab her ass and push her up the wall, burying my face between her legs. "Just gotta let go."

"Jesus, where'd you learn to do that?" she moans.

"Don't ask questions you don't want to know the answer to," I mumble, and then continue eating her out.

Her fingers claw at me as I push her to her limit, sucking

and licking my way to her orgasm. I love the sounds she makes, interrupted only by desperate breaths and quivers. She's unlike any girl I've had before. So inexperienced, but eager to learn. And it turns me on like nothing else can.

My cock is about to burst from my pants, so I growl, "Come. Now. Before I shove my cock up your pussy and make you come."

"Fuck!" she yells.

And I can feel her explode in my mouth.

She quakes in my arms, her whole body rocking up and down as she grinds on my face. All her delicious juices drip down, and I moan from the taste. So fucking good, it riles me up like no tomorrow.

I lower her and immediately smash my mouth to hers.

She seems surprised, as her eyes are still wide open when I take my lips off hers.

"Wow ..."

"What?"

"I've never ... come that fast. Or against a wall."

I raise a brow. "Never?"

"Well, the rabbit did it once."

"Rabbit ... you don't mean like a vibrator, do you?"

"Yeah ..." She smashes her lips together.

I laugh. "I'm no fucking rabbit, although I do fuck like one."

"I hope not. I don't like vibrating sticks in my pussy, only on my clit."

I wrap my arm around her and pull her close. "Well, when I'm done with you, you'll like anything I give you, wherever I give it to you."

"I'm already sold. I know you can fuck me the right

way."

"What gave it away?" I smile cheekily.

"Your arrogant talk." She raises a brow.

I lean in and whisper in her ear. "Don't tell me you don't like it because I won't believe it."

She eyes me sideways. "You're right. But your cock had better be just as good as your tongue."

I narrow my eyes. "They don't call this the love stick for nothing …"

She laughs, and when I hear her awkward snort, I laugh too.

"Sorry," she mumbles.

"Don't be. Kinda breaks the ice, doesn't it?"

"Yeah, except it already broke when you stuck your tongue in my pussy."

I wink. "And I'd do it all over again." I swiftly spin her in my arms. "But my cock can't wait any longer."

She squeals a little as I grab her hands and put them behind her back.

"What are you doing?" she asks.

"I like things my way …" I unfurl my tie and wrap it around her wrists. "And I like things tied up."

She gulps. "And then?"

"Then I fuck your wet pussy from behind until I come."

"Hmm …" She shivers with delight.

"Did I just hear you moan?" I say.

"Maybe …"

"You like being tied up by strangers?" I ask, pulling her bonds tighter. She jolts a little but only seems more excited. "Aren't you scared?"

"Do you want an honest answer or a lie?"

I smile as I whisper, "You're my kind of crazy."

She bites her lip, but then a gasp escapes her mouth as I smack her ass.

"You know what else I like? This ass."

I slap it again, making her jolt up and down against the wall.

"Fuck ..."

"Painful?"

"No ..." she murmurs, clasping her legs together, which tells me her pussy responds to the pain in a good way. Fuck. Could this girl be any more perfect? I don't ever fuck a girl twice, but with her ... I might think about it.

"Good because I enjoy seeing a red ass. It matches your hair well." I pull on her wrists and bend her over so her ass is pointing toward me. Then I zip down my pants and take out my cock. I pull a condom from my pocket and rip it open with my mouth, spitting away the plastic as I wrap the latex around my hard-on.

As my tip touches her entrance, she hisses a little, almost like she's preparing for me to thrust. But I don't like it when she's prepared.

I slide my cock along her slit, extending the time she'll have to wait. Her moans grow increasingly louder as I tease her to the limit. My balls are bursting with cum, but I can wait ... until she least expects it.

One hard smack to the ass has her almost standing straight again, but I push her back down.

"Don't move," I growl. "Take it like a good girl."

"You're one kinky motherfucker, aren't you?"

I smack her other ass cheek. "That's for the filthy talk."

"Oh ... so you like to punish, huh?"

I fondle her clit while my cock is still erect against her pussy. "As I said, I like to get what I want, and what I want is to fuck you without having to control myself."

"Don't …" she murmurs.

"Don't what?"

"Don't hold back."

Fuck. Me.

Now, she's gone and done it.

Without saying a word, I thrust into her pussy completely, making her gasp out loud.

A cry follows as my cock pulses inside her, and then I pull out again … only to thrust again.

I repeat this over and over again, fully claiming her pussy, her moans and gasps filling the room.

"Louder," I growl, as I pump into her. "I want to hear you scream."

"Fuck!" she yells.

I slap her ass again, the sudden sizzle making her jolt up.

I use the opportunity to grab one of her tits and toy with it, taking her nipple between my index finger and thumb, rolling it around. Her body is hot against mine, sweat dripping down her back as I fuck her hard and without mercy.

She knows as well as I do how reckless this is. But nothing's more exciting than being reckless, especially when it comes to sex.

"Please …" she moans.

"Please, what?" I pant into her ear.

Fondling her tits makes her pussy thump, and I get the sense that she's close.

So I hold her wrists as reins as I fuck her from behind as

fast and hard as I can. My own release isn't the only thing I'm seeking. I want her to make me come.

I flick her clit while ravaging her. "Don't fight it. Come from my cock fucking your tiny hole, girl."

"Oh, god ..." she moans, her pussy tightening around me.

"Yes, come all over me," I growl.

When I feel it, I combust.

A loud, drawn-out roar emanates from my mouth as I plunge into her, feeling her clamp around me. My seed jets out in a seemingly never-ending spurt. My toes curl from the intensity, my nails digging into her skin as I hold her wrists tight.

When my cock deflates, I pull out and lean against her back, panting heavily.

"Wow ..." she murmurs.

I press a soft kiss to the back of her neck and then untie her wrists.

"Thanks," she says.

"My pleasure. Literally." I smirk as I take off the condom, tie it in a knot, and throw it in the bin.

I zip up again as she pulls up her panties and plucks her bra from the floor.

"What now?" she asks.

"Now ... nothing." I shrug as I walk to my kitchen and start some coffee. She keeps looking at me, a bit befuddled. "You're welcome to shower," I add.

"Thanks." She nods, and then saunters off.

She opens a door, and I immediately hear lots of clattering sticks and metal.

"The other door," I say.

"Oops. Sorry." She laughs, and I hear her try to pick them up.

"No worries."

"Right." She clears her throat. "I broke your broom. What do you want me to do with it?"

She shows me two ends of a stick, one still has the brush on it.

I smirk to myself as my mind overflows with things to say, and I pick the most horrible one. "Paint it pink and tape a vibrator to it."

She makes a weird, creeped-out face, followed by an annoyed one. I open my mouth to tell her to throw it away instead, but she responds. "Don't dare me because I *will* do it."

I shrug, smiling. Guess I don't even have to bother. "Cool. Keep it then."

She narrows her eyes and then storms off.

After a few seconds, I hear the shower running, and I smile to myself. I don't think this girl really knew what she was doing, after all. She seems clueless, yet it's kind of endearing too. Not that it matters because I probably won't ever see her again.

When she's done showering, I place two cups of coffee on the counter and wait for her to step out. She's still in her bra and panties as she walks over to me.

"Don't want to put your clothes back on?" I ask, raising my brows.

"Too hot."

"Then I guess you don't want this either." I attempt to pull the cup of coffee away, but she grabs it before I can.

"I'll take it," she muses, our eyes locking for the first

time since we had sex.

She blushes and pulls the cup away, almost as if she's afraid to touch my fingers.

I sigh. Time to pull out the big guns. "Look, I know this is awkward, but it doesn't have to be," I say. "It was just sex."

"Just sex," she repeats as if it's a mantra to herself.

"Right, and it doesn't mean anything."

"Meaningless sex." Her eyes drift off a little as she takes a sip of her coffee.

"Doesn't mean it wasn't good," I say, taking a sip too. "You tell me."

She glances at me and then looks away again.

"Or not. It doesn't matter. As long as you don't regret it."

"No," she says, looking straight at me. "I don't regret it. It's just … the first time I've ever done this."

"What? Just sex?"

"Yeah. Just sex. No boyfriend. No date. No nothing."

I smile as I put my cup down. "And did you like it?"

A wicked, dirty smile creeps onto her lips. "A lot."

I grin. "Good. Just remember that."

After she drinks her coffee, she gets up and collects her clothes, putting them on again with ease. I watch her from a distance as she makes her way to my door. I hesitate to follow her and open it for her, but I know it'll only make it more difficult, so I don't.

"Thanks for the coffee," she says as her hand rests on the door handle. "And for the sex. Oh, and for the broom, of course." She grins playfully as she grabs the broken broom off the floor.

I laugh and wink. "You're welcome, I guess."

She nods, flicking her hair back as she opens the door. "See ya. Or not."

"Or not," I repeat.

Not is what I usually say … but, for some reason, looking at her leave gives me the shivers. Like I'm supposed to say something. Like I'm supposed to make her stop and ask for her number. Or at least ask her to come back sometime.

I don't know why. I never have this thought with any girl.

But then the moment disappears as she closes the door behind her and sucks all the hotness out of the room in an instant. I walk to the door and listen as she walks away. Her wedges are the last thing I hear clicking in the dark before I turn around and walk away, repeating my mantra over and over in my head.

Walk away, Thomas, walk away.
Don't get attached.
Don't ever get to know them.
Don't ever fall in love again.

Chapter 2

Hailey

I tiptoe into my dorm room and close the door without making a sound. My roomie, Lesley, is sprawled facedown on her bed. One of her feet almost touches the floor, and I can hear her snore. Containing my laughter, I go to my bed and quickly undress to hop under the warm blanket.

Smiling to myself, I can't stop thinking about what I just did.

Sneaking out to dance in the middle of the night.

It's so not what I usually do, but it was definitely worth it.

Fuck. I just fucked.

For the very first time.

And Jesus, it was just as amazing as Lesley says it is.

Although I don't think she got tied up. Or tongue-fucked right before.

God, it was amazing, and all I wanna do is scream, but that would make me an asshole for waking her up, so I don't.

I'm no longer a freaking virgin. Fucking finally.

***

The next morning

I don't think I've ever slept this well. At least not while sleeping with that snore whore next to me. I smile stupidly as I put on my clothes and look at myself in the mirror, thinking 'fuck yeah, this bitch got laid!' Then I pack my bag for the first day of the second semester at college.

Yes, I know it's seriously fucked up, but I really didn't wanna end up in class being the only virgin. And I can now honestly say I am in love with dick. Maybe I'll become a junkie. Beats getting drunk at a party any day.

I look in our private bathroom, trying to find Lesley, but she seems to have disappeared on me.

"If you aren't coming back, I'm going without you, Les," I shout.

Then I turn around and sling my backpack over my shoulder. Right as I try to leave through the door, it slams in my face.

"Why?" Lesley's behind the door. With my vibrator in her hand. "Why?" She jiggles it like it's fucking jelly.

"Why what? Why the fuck are you holding Mr. Pink?"

"Mr. Pink?" She snorts. "That's what you call him?"

"You're just fucking jealous." I try to snatch it away from her. "Get your own."

"Ew, I don't want your stinky stick." She only holds it with her index finger and thumb now, swaying it back and forth but still keeping it away from me.

"Then give it back."

"No, not before you tell me. Why ... was this not under your bed?" she asks.

I frown. "What?"

"It's always under your bed. I know you're a vib-whore. You use this thing on a daily basis."

"What? Nah ..." I try to hide my blush by reaching for the vibrator, but it isn't working.

"Yeah, you do. I can hear the noise." She raises her brow. "The thing is ... I *didn't* last night."

"So?" I put my hand against my side.

She narrows her eyes at me. "You weren't here last night ..."

"Maybe I was, maybe I wasn't."

"Spill it!" she says, pointing the vibrator at me like it's some sort of correctional tool.

"Fuck no, my business."

"You're glowing ... You're hiding something. Friends don't hide stuff ..." she says. "I'm not letting you leave."

"We'll miss class," I say, folding my arms.

She shrugs. "Don't care."

"First day? Hello?"

She shrugs again.

I sigh. "Fine! I was out. Happy now?"

She pouts. "Without me? You never go without me. Oh, no ... don't tell me it's because of your mom ... What happened?"

I shake my head. "No, it's not because of my mom. I just wanted to see what it was like on my own." Now, I feel guilty.

She shakes her head. "Idiot. You could've been drugged."

"I know, and I'm sorry; it was stupid."

"Damn right. Why'd you go alone?"

"I just wanted to dance with some guys without making a scene—"

"You mean, without me cock-blocking you. Yeah, I get it." She shrugs.

"No, not like that ... I just didn't want you to be left alone in there while I went off with some dude."

"Oh ... that's it." She grins from ear to ear. "You actually managed to hook up with a guy, didn't you?"

My eyes widen. "How do—"

Her jaw drops. "Oh, my god ..."

Shit. She lured it out of me.

"Fuck you!" I smack her on the arm.

"I didn't think you'd actually admit it so fast. Oh, my god! You were with a guy!"

"Not. That. Special." I smack her again.

"It is when you were there in the middle of the fucking night. Yeah, I heard you sneaking in."

"So?"

"You did it, didn't you?" she says, almost hanging on my lips for the answer.

"If I tell you, will you shut up?"

"Maybe."

I roll my eyes. "Yeah, we fucked."

"Fuck, yes!" she screams. "Finally! I'm not alone anymore."

I shake my head. "Oh, Jesus."

"What? It's lonely in ho-land. Now, I've finally got my best friend with me." She hugs me tight. "So how was it? And who? Where? Tell me everything."

"We have ten minutes to get to class!" I say.

"So? Just tell me the small details. Quick." She pokes me with the vibrator. "We're not leaving. This is too important. Spill it."

"Fine." I laugh a little. "He was a bit older than me, but not much."

"How old?"

"I don't know … maybe twenty-five?"

"How can you not know?" She makes a face.

"I don't know."

"You don't know anything about him? What about his name?"

I shake my head. She looks at me as if I've been smoking crack.

"Are you insane? You slept with a dude for the first fucking time, and you don't even know his name? You gave away your fucking virginity to a random stranger?"

"That pretty much sums it up." I shrug. "It's not a big deal."

"Of course, it is!" She grabs me. "You finally lost your V-card."

"I don't want it to be a big deal. That's why I did it. I just wanted to do it. That's it."

"Damn, girl …" She lets out a short gasp. "Can't believe it." She makes a sad face. "My little Hailey, all grown up."

I wave away her hand as she tries to pat me on the head. "Fuck you, Les."

"Oh, c'mon. I'm just proud of you. And I can't believe you did something that dangerous." She puts her arm around my shoulder. "Sneaking off with some random stranger. Was it good?"

I smile just thinking about it. "Oh, yeah ... good."

"Like good good? Like *so good Fabio would be jealous of our fuck that came straight out of a romance novel* or *Gooooooood so fucking good I just came from his voice alone*?" She fans herself.

"Last one." I smirk.

She squeals. "Where'd you guys meet?"

"Just a club ..."

"Why didn't you bring me? Maybe he could've introduced me to some of his friends."

"We were both alone."

"So he was on the lookout for a chick to bang. I get it. Nothing wrong with that."

"Exactly," I say. "We just wanted to fuck. End of story."

"Except it was your first time. Well done, girl." She kisses me on the cheek. "Feel any different?"

"No, not really. I thought I would ... but I don't."

"Heh, that's what we all think. Just revel in the fact that your banging was awesome. Not all of us are so lucky." She jiggles Mr. Pink back and forth again. "Right, Mr. Pinky-Dink?"

"Oh, fuck off." I snatch the vibrator from her hand and throw it backward onto my bed. "Let's just fucking go and get this first day of second semester over with."

"Fine, fine, but after class, can we look him up on Facebook? Please?" she begs.

"No. Besides, I don't know anything about him. I wouldn't even know where to start."

"Fuck. Such a shame if he was *that* good."

"I have nothing to compare it with, but what I can tell you is that he was much better than any of the boys who ever tried to touch me there. Or anywhere, for that matter."

"Well, good; you seemed like you needed it, from the number of batteries you've wasted on Mr. Pinky-Wink." She pokes me in the side and grins. "Now, let's go troll some classes."

***

Minutes later

We shuffle into class behind all the other students and sit down on two seats at the end of the second to the last row. The class is noisy—a lot of students chatting and some even throwing stuff around.

"Jesus, they're so loud," Lesley shouts.

"I know, right?" I yell back.

"I wonder where the teacher is." She stands up and looks around, gaping at all the doors, but only students seem to pour in.

Then a girl sitting a few rows in front of us draws her attention. "Layla!" She waves and the girl gets up to shout back.

I start unpacking my books while Lesley continues to shout back and forth with the girl. I won't butt in since I don't know Layla. Besides, I like being in my own little bubble from time to time.

Suddenly, the door slams and a draft of air swooshes through as a man in a suit passes my seat. I look up as he saunters down the steps, the room growing quiet with his arrival.

Lesley sits down as the man apparently has the ability to silence every student in the room just with his presence. She pokes me in the side with her elbow and nods at him. "Nice ass," she whispers to me. "For a teacher."

I grin and shake my head.

The man sets his briefcase down next to the table in the middle of the room and walks to the whiteboard. He picks up a marker and starts writing. I can literally hear the swipes. It's that quiet as he writes down the name of his class.

Hospitality & Marketing Basics

Meanwhile, the class has become a little noisy with whispers, and I catch some from the seats above.

"He's the new professor, isn't he?"

"Yeah, he looks so handsome!" someone whispers.

"He can hear you," another one says.

The man suddenly slams his marker back on the board, making me jolt in my seat.

The room is completely quiet again.

That's when he turns around. "Welcome to class, everyone. My name is Thomas Hard, and I'll be teaching you how to market your business or product, and how to keep your customers very, *very* happy."

My classmates are giggling at his name, but I can't.

I'm nailed to my seat, frozen, as I stare at the man in front of me.

That man …

Sexy as fuck. Hair short, slick, with just the right amount of edge. Scruffy jaw, cut to perfection. Plump, lickable lips shaped in a small but tempting smile.

Buffed, but not too buff, and all suited up.

Completely different from what I remember.

I suck in a breath as his eyes go around the class. I can't look away, even though I want to. Desperately. Especially when his navy-blue eyes lock with mine.

Fuck no.

I scramble my books together and shove them back in my bag, leaving a few pens behind as I jump up from my seat.

"Where are you going?" Lesley asks.

"I gotta go."

I rush up the steps, and the students I pass suddenly look at me instead of him, but I don't care. I storm out the door without looking back. I can't, even if I wanted to.

I run away as far as I can until I'm alone in a hallway, where I prop myself up against a pillar and drop my bag on the floor. My heart is racing. My eyes are closed.

I can't unsee what I just saw.

That man … it's *him*.

The man I had sex with last night is my teacher.

Chapter 3

Hailey

I go into the bathroom and stare at myself in the mirror. God, I look like a fucking mess.

I turn on the faucet and stick my hands under the water. They're shaking. I quickly splash my face with the cold water, hoping it'll rinse away the shame.

It doesn't.

It's almost as if it's visible on my face. Like you could literally walk up to me without knowing me and say, 'Hey, you're that girl who slept with her professor without knowing it, aren't you?'

I'm now *that* girl.

That girl who not only spent her first fuck on a man she never met … but did it with her professor.

That girl who royally fucked up.

Fucking hell.

I slap myself in the face and murmur, "Get a hold of yourself, Hailey."

I don't know why, but it helps.

No one knows we did it. Lesley knows I fucked some random dude, but she doesn't know it was him. But fuck, I hope none of this gets out because that would mean the end of my staying-low-at-school style.

Yes, I might be the red-haired girl, the nose-piercing girl, the vibrator-under-the-bed girl, the girl who loves ice cream and rock music, who likes glitter, unicorns, and rainbows and black all together, the girl who's a mess and a mesh of all things both disgusting and fancy.

But I like who I am, and I like my privacy. So I need to make sure I keep my shit private.

Slinging my bag over my shoulder, I storm outside. I find a nice spot near a tree and take a packet of cigarettes from my pocket. I light one up and take a much-needed smoke break. Then I put my earbuds in and listen to "Kitty Hawk" by Ki: Theory.

I stay here for a good half an hour, enjoying a bottle of orange juice while reading a magazine. I know, corny, but I have to do something to take my mind off the whole thing, and I know going back to my dorm room won't help.

I hear shuffling behind me in the sand, and when I turn my head, someone shouts in my face.

"Where the fuck did you go?" Lesley asks.

"Here," I say, smiling like an idiot.

She smacks me on the head with an empty bottle of water. "Asshole. You left me in there. Alone."

"You have plenty of friends."

"So? You're my best friend. You can't just storm out. We were in the middle of class."

I shrug. "I felt sick, so I went to the bathroom," I lie.

Best friend.

What does that mean when I lie to her face?

I don't even know anymore. We used to be so close, since way back when we met on the first day of college. If I knew then that I'd be lying to her face, I'd have punched myself. But I can't exactly tell her the truth either. What I did with Thomas was a big fat no-no. I can't tell anyone. Not even her.

I don't want her to know. Yet. Maybe not ever. I don't know.

This isn't just something you tell someone while you're casually sitting under a tree.

"And what the fuck is that?" She snatches the magazine from my hand. "*Playboy*?"

"Found it in the trash."

"Trash? You're outta your mind." She throws it back at me.

"What? I just needed some distraction. It wasn't covered in filth or anything ... except on the inside." I grin.

"You're a lunatic," she says, sitting down beside me.

"And proud of it."

"So you ran out because you needed to puke? I don't believe it. You never get sick on the first day. You're never nervous."

"Today, I was. I can't help it. Can we just talk about something else?"

"As long as you promise me this isn't because of your

mom."

"It isn't."

"Are you sure?" She places a hand on my shoulder. "Because you know you can tell me everything, right?"

"Yeah … No, it's not my mom. I promise."

"Okay. So you left class because you were sick. Were you too embarrassed to come back?"

I look at her, nodding. "Yeah."

"I get it. Everyone was looking at you when you rushed out."

I groan, palming my face. "Please don't remind me."

She laughs a bit. "It's okay. No one will remember. They all only had eyes for the teacher. He's freakishly hot."

"Tell me about it …" I say, choking up a little at the thought of seeing him again.

"Just as long as you don't leave me in there again. We're best friends. Best friends stick together." She rubs me and then gets up again. "Wanna get a Blizzard at Dairy Queen?"

"Fuck, yes," I say, as I get up from the ground and brush the dirt off. "No fucking sickness can stop me from licking that ice cream."

She grins. "*Nothing* stops *you* from licking ice cream. I've seen you lick it off some guy's abs at a party. You'd do pretty much anything for it."

"Damn right, I would. And who cares about abs anyway? I just wanted the ice cream."

She holds up her hand. "High five!" And I slap hers. "Now, let's go get some ice cream."

★★★

That same night

Hours later, Lesley drags me to a club, but when I see where she's taking me, I stop in my tracks.

"Oh, no … I've changed my mind."

"Why?" She grabs my hand. "Nothing's wrong with this place."

"I know. I'm just … Can't we just go watch a movie or something?"

She seems flabbergasted, but then she laughs. "Stop joking around. Let's go have some fun. You obviously need it."

I guess that's what happens when you tell your best friend you got sick from being nervous. Of course, it's a lie, but she doesn't know, and she thinks this place will make me relax.

Unfortunately, it's the same place I met Mr. Thomas Hard.

"C'mon, it can't be that bad," she says, pulling me along. "I'm here. That's more than you need to have fun." She playfully sticks out her tongue as she drags me through the doors.

"Fine," I mumble as she gives me a stern look.

"Yay! I'm buying," she cheers, as we walk to the bar. "Two tequilas, please."

"Aren't you two a bit too young for this place?" The bartender narrows his eyes.

With a smug smile, Lesley pulls out her ID and shows it to him. With suspicion, he checks it but doesn't say a word.

Lesley purses her lips. "I'm the good kind of young. The legal-but-still-smoking-hot kind of young."

"And her?" The bartender looks at me now.

Lesley eyes me. "C'mon, Hailey, show him." She winks.

I reach into my pocket and pull out my card. He inspects it thoroughly, almost as if he sees something.

"All right. Two tequilas coming up." He walks off, and I breathe a sigh of relief.

Lesley leans sideways. "I told you it would work," she whispers. "These cards are magic!"

"I'm so glad I didn't need it last time," I whisper. "And I'm sure as hell glad he didn't notice they were fake. But what if we get caught next time?"

"We won't," she says. "Not when you've got these lips and these eyes to lie our way through it." She points at her own face, then her tits. "I mean, who can resist this?"

I laugh a little. "Big head much?"

"Not at all, actually," she muses, shrugging.

I shove her, and she almost falls off her stool. "Whoa!"

"Sorry," I say, still laughing. "No, I'm not."

"Of course, you aren't. Be careful, or I'mma hook you up with the nearest old guy."

"Please don't," I say, making a face. "I've had enough of men for a while."

"Oh, so he was old?" she says, narrowing her eyes.

"I didn't say that."

"I can see when you're lying, Hailey," she says, smirking. "But he probably wasn't that old. Fifty. Forty? Thirty?" When my eye twitches, she says, "AH-HA!"

"Here are your drinks," the bartender interrupts, placing two glasses in front of us.

I quickly pick it up and take a sip.

"So he's a thirty-something hot guy."

"I didn't say anything," I say, coughing because the drink burns my throat.

"You don't need to. I can read your face like a book."

I raise my brow. "Do I look like a Harlequin romance?"

She picks up her tequila. "No, more like a *Fifty Shades of Grey*."

My eyes widen.

"Oh, god." She almost spits out her drink but manages to swallow it, then slams her glass down. "You're kidding. It is? He was like Grey? Did he spank you? Tie you up?"

"Shhhh!" I say.

"What? It's not like anyone can hear us with this music blasting through the speakers," she says. "C'mon, I wanna know. Give me the good stuff. My own sex life sucks."

"Like mine is so great. I only did it with one guy."

"Yeah, but he was smoking hot, and you guys did kinky stuff, didn't you? I mean, that's definitely worth talking about and swooning over." She sucks on her lip. "C'mon, Hailey, I won't tell a soul, I promise."

"You promise?" I lower my eyes.

"Pinky swear on my current non-existent sex life." She holds up her pinky and shakes mine.

"Fine, yes, he was in his thirties, and the sex was straight up kinky."

She squeals. Too late do I cover her mouth with my hand. "Stop yelling!"

"I can't. It's too fucking cool. Like you literally went from zero to a hundred in terms of sex."

"I know, but just keep it between us, okay?"

"I promise, but you gotta stop feeling ashamed." She places her hand on my upper arm. "There's nothing wrong with having sex, and there's nothing wrong with talking about it." She smiles. "So ... what did he do?"

I grab my tequila and take another sip as she hangs on my lips. "Well, he kind of tied me up... and spanked me."

"Both? Oh, my god." She fans herself, grabbing her tequila. "I definitely need this drink now."

"Okay, enough about him. How was class? Did I miss anything?"

"Miss anything? Well, apart from his cute booty ... no, I don't think so."

I sigh out loud and shake my head. "You didn't pay attention, did you? You just stared at his ass."

"What?" She shrugs. "I can't help it. If there's good ass, I need to study it. They should give me points for that. In fact, an entire class should be dedicated to judging butts all day long. I'd fucking ace it."

I chuckle. "Yeah, that's enough tequila for you, Les." I try to take away her glass, but she isn't having it.

"No, I think I'll have another one."

"Let's just dance," I say.

She pulls the glass back so hard, the contents spill over and onto her shirt. "Ugh! Look at this. Now, I'm all wet."

"That's probably the first time in weeks," I muse, and she gasps, then slaps my arm.

"Not funny, bitch. And for the record, I had sex"—she clears her throat—"last week." She pulls my arm and drags me off my stool. "C'mon, we're going to the toilet, and you're gonna help me clean up."

We go into the bathroom, where I grab a few pieces of toilet paper, and she pulls off her shirt. "No one here anyway," she says as she holds her shirt above the sink and squeezes out the liquid.

"Here." I hand her the toilet paper. "I don't have anything else."

"This is fine," she says, dabbing them into the wet spots. "It'll have to do." When she's done, she says, "Can you wait a minute? I need to use the bathroom."

"Sure."

I stay near the sink, while she goes into a stall.

And then I literally hear the biggest fart in the entire fucking world.

"What the fuck," I mumble.

"Sorry." She giggles out loud, and another fart comes out. "Fuck, I think this is gonna be a smelly one."

"Okay, I'm gonna wait outside," I say, laughing my ass off.

"I'm dying!" I hear a painful moan and then another fart, which is my cue to go.

As I walk out, I take out my cell phone to check the time, but when I put it back in my pocket, I bump into someone.

"Shit, sorry."

"No problem."

Fuck.

That.

Voice.

It's as if fate is sticking its middle finger in my face right now.

This can't happen twice, can it? Yes, it fucking can, because *he* is standing in front of me. Again.

Thomas fucking Hard.

Boy, is he hard to avoid.

Chapter 4

THOMAS

Of all the people I run in to ... this girl shows up?

I never expected to see her again in this joint ... let alone in my classroom.

The girl I fucked last night is my fucking student.

It can't get any more fucked up than that.

"Well," I say, clearing my throat, "this is awkward."

"Yeah ..." She tucks her red hair behind her ear, and I can't help but look at her mouth as she sucks on her bottom lip. They still look kissable as hell.

Fuck me; this is messed up

"Aren't you my student?" I ask, narrowing my eyes.

"I think so," she says.

"I saw you in class yesterday." I cock my head. "You

were the one who ran."

Her cheeks stain red. Not that I didn't already know who she was. I just want her to know that I know it was her.

And I know exactly why she ran too.

"You didn't know I was your teacher," I say.

She slams her lips shut and looks away.

"You had sex with your teacher," I mumble under a heavy breath.

She suddenly grabs my shirt and pulls herself up to eye level. "Forget about it. Please."

I smirk and shake my head. "Forget about it? How? I can't exactly erase your body from my mind." I grab her hands and push them away until I have her backed against the wall. "You know, I've been thinking about you. From the moment you showed up in my classroom, I knew I was fucked."

"You? You mean me!" she says.

I place a hand on the wall behind her. "*We* fucked up. But I could never *forget* about you."

Her breathing picks up, and she swallows as my eyes drift over her outfit. She's wearing a little black dress with high heels, and her hair is brushed back. Not as raunchy as when I met her, but still very sexy. Too sexy.

"What are you doing here?" I ask.

"None of your business." She glowers. "Why are you here anyway?"

"Why would I tell you if you won't tell me?" I raise my brows.

"Whatever." She rolls her eyes. "Let's just forget this ever happened."

"No, I don't think so. I know your name now." Her

eyes flicker with bewilderment. Yeah, I know because I checked my list the moment I saw her in my class. And maybe I asked around a little. I lick my bottom lip, wondering how she'll react. "Hailey Walters."

I take my time pronouncing her name because I want to do it right. It rolls nicely off my tongue, like something I could get used to saying a lot.

"Doesn't mean jack shit."

"You like filthy words, don't you?" I muse. "I could teach you a few more."

Her lips part, but no sound comes out.

"Speechless?" I muse.

"Oh, please ... stop acting like you're all that."

"Likewise," I say.

"Yeah, well, I just used you to get rid of my virgin status," she boasts.

Completely catching me by surprise.

My jaw drops, and I'm inclined to shout, but then I realize we're in a public place, and I really don't want to make a scene. Especially not considering she's one of my students.

I shake my head and close my eyes, sighing. "You were a virgin?"

She shushes me. "Not so loud."

"Right ... Well, fuck me."

If that's the truth, then Jesus.

I really fucked up.

I not only banged a student, she was a virgin too.

Well, it's too late to change that now. Guess knowing is just an added bonus. Hurray.

With half-mast eyes, I think about my situation. "I

should've seen this coming."

"Duh."

My brow rises. "Do you always act like this to your teachers?"

"You're not just a teacher ... Professor."

"Not Professor, please. It makes me feel old. Teacher is fine," I correct. "And you're not just a student ... not anymore." I lower my head. "Are you even old enough to be here?"

"I am if I want to be."

The left corner of my lip quirks up into a smile. "Attitude. We'll need to fix that."

The ladies' room door opens, and I quickly step away from Hailey.

"Oh ... hey, aren't you ... Mr. Hard." It's that girl who sat next to Hailey during class. They must've come here together.

"Hi, Lesley."

"Oh, you know my name? I'm flattered."

"Of course, I do." I smirk.

Hailey signals Lesley to cut it out, but she doesn't see it ... I do, and it makes me smile.

"I didn't expect to see you here," Lesley says.

"Neither did I when I saw the two of you."

"Yeah, well, this place is the bomb, you know. How could we not go here?" She giggles.

I frown. "Right."

"Okay, time to go." Hailey tries to jerk Lesley's arm, but she isn't having it.

"Oh, it's fine. I'll excuse myself," I say, winking at Hailey as I step back. "I didn't know this place was a regular for students. Guess I need to find a new spot." I turn around and give them a short wave. "See you in class, girls."

***

Hailey

That bastard.

How dare he shove me against the wall? How dare he get up in my face like that? And more importantly, how dare he get me fucking riled up over seeing his fine ass?

Fuck.

Out of all the people I could run into, it had to be him.

He probably comes here often. I should've thought of it. But still … he could've known I'd be here too. I mean we fucking met here, for crying out loud. One of us should've been the smart one. Guess it was neither.

"Did you see his ass?" Lesley says.

"Oh, shut up," I say.

She sneers, "Geez, what's gotten into you?"

"Him. Under my skin."

"Why?"

"Didn't you hear what he said? That he was gonna find another place to chill because of us?" I say.

"So? What teacher would want to hang out at the same place as his students?"

"He made it sound like we were scum!"

She grabs my arm. "Hailey, I think you're making a big deal out of nothing."

"No, let me go." I jerk away from her hold.

"Hailey ... c'mon, can't we just forget about him and go have some fun?"

I frown, looking at the dance floor, but knowing he was here too, lecturing me about what I should and shouldn't do makes me mad, and I don't like being mad. Or maybe I'm just pissed off because he suddenly appeared back in my life when I thought I'd never see him again ... and it turns out that thought was a blissful lie.

I make a face. "I don't know."

She pouts. "Aw ... but we haven't even checked out the guys yet. Maybe there's a cute one on the dance floor just right for you. Nothing like getting out of a funk by banging another dude."

"I think I'd rather just go home. Do you mind?"

She looks at me and sighs. "Something's wrong."

"Nah, I'm fine." I give her a fake smile.

"Don't believe it."

"Okay, it's the tequila. Happy now?" I say. "I just wanna go home and read a book or something. Can we do that?"

"A book or something? You? Reading a book?" She snorts.

I bring my fingers to her face and press her lips together. "Zip it!"

"Hmm," she murmurs, and I release her. "Fine. Okay. We'll go."

"Great."

"But you sure as hell won't be reading a book." She grabs my hand. "If we're going home, we're gonna look up Mr. Sexy on Facebook."

"Oh, god ..." I slap myself in the face because I just

know this is going to be so cringe-worthy.

"And then we're gonna watch *Sex & the City*, for old time's sake."

"Seriously?" I say as we walk out of the club.

"Honey, I need sex. I don't care where, but if I'm not getting any, at least let me watch someone else get it. Okay?"

"We could watch porn," I say.

She opens her mouth but then closes it again, her brow lifting curiously. Then she nods slowly and smiles brightly. "Good idea, let's do that. I call dibs on James Deen!"

Chapter 5

Hailey

Later that night

I open the door to my mom's house and find her lying on the floor near the couch. A puddle of blood pools around her head, and her eyes are wide open. I run to her as fast as I can. "Mom!" I shout, but she doesn't respond.

Her body is lifeless as I pick her up and hold her close to me. Tears run down my cheeks, and when I look at my hands, they're soaked in blood. My breathing stops the moment I see the gaping hole in her heart.

A door to the left slams open and in comes a man carrying a rifle. "What are you doing here?"

He holds it up and points it at me.

A scream as loud as the gunshot that follows erupts from my

lungs.

I sit up straight in bed. Heart pounding, I have sweat dripping down my forehead.

I touch my skin, but there's no hole. I look at my hands and see no blood.

Then I touch my face ... tears all over.

"What's wrong?" Lesley asks, as she gets up from her bed and sits down beside me. "Are you okay?" She puts her hand on my forehead. "You're burning up."

"I'm fine," I lie.

I'm not.

I'm not fine at all, but what am I supposed to tell her?

They're just nightmares. That's it.

"You were dreaming again, weren't you?" she asks.

I nod slowly, and she grabs my hand and squeezes it tightly. "If you wanna talk about it, I'm here."

"I just ... keep seeing *him*," I say, biting my lip to test if I'm really awake.

"Your mother's new boyfriend?"

"Yeah, but he's holding a shotgun, and—" I choke up.

Lesley grabs me and pulls me toward her, hugging me tight. "It was only a dream. Just remember that."

"I know, but what if it becomes the truth? What if these are all warning signs, and I'm ignoring them?"

"You're not psychic, Hailey. No one can predict the future."

"But I can't let anything happen to her."

She pushes me away so she can look me in the eye. "She'll be fine. She's a grown woman; she can handle it. And if you're unsure, call her."

I take in a breath and then grab my cell phone and dial

my mom's number. "Mom?" I say as someone picks up.

"You again?" It's him. "You dare to call us after leaving your mom like that? No. You show your face first, then we talk." Before I can reply, the phone's cut off.

I pull the phone away from my ear and stare at it like I can't believe he just did that.

"What happened?" Lesley asks.

"*He* picked up," I say.

"Oh … fuck."

In a fit, I throw the phone. It ends up against the wall, probably broken to bits.

"Damn, Hailey." Lesley picks up the phone and shows me the screen, which is cracked. "Why'd you have to do that?"

I shrug. I don't wanna think. I don't wanna know. I just want to disappear.

"Hailey?" She snaps her fingers. "Earth to Hailey."

I get up from the bed. "Let's just get ready for class."

That's the last I speak of it.

Every time she brings it up, I change the subject until she understands that I really don't wanna talk about it. I don't wanna make her feel bad, so I don't tell her directly. I know she cares about me. There's just no way she, or anyone else, can help my mom or me.

I have a few options, and one of which is ignoring it until the pain goes away.

I always choose that option. It seems like the easiest one.

That, or getting wasted.

Just as long as I can forget.

***

Years ago

I stare at the bird in the tree, chirping as hard as he can. I wonder why he does that. If he feels lost. If he's alone and afraid. Like me.

The grass tickles my toes as I inch closer on my flip-flops, trying not to scare it. I just wanna have a closer look, that's all. I love staring at things, animals in particular. They're so vibrant, so alive. Unlike me.

Unlike everything I've experienced recently. I wonder if Mom feels the same.

"What are you looking at?" Mom shouts, interrupting my thoughts.

"Shh!" I whisper, turning my head toward her. "You'll scare it away." I slowly point at the bird as she comes to stand behind me.

"A bird?"

"Yeah ... it's constantly singing. Why do you think it does that?" I ask.

"Maybe it's looking for a mate," my mom says, chuckling.

"Aww ... so he is lonely ..." I frown and rub my lips together.

Mom places her hand on my shoulder. "Don't worry. I'm sure there's another female bird in the neighborhood."

"How do you know?" I ask.

"Well, I don't know why. I just know it."

I sigh. "Everything that lives eventually dies. Everyone will feel the heartbreak. Even that bird."

She bends over and says, "Oh, Hailey …"

"It's the truth, isn't it?"

"Yes, but …" She smiles. "Every human and animal should be grateful for every second they spend here on earth. Life isn't a guarantee, it's a gift we should cherish. Just like love."

"It's over before you know it," I mutter, still staring at the bird as it flutters away into the distance. "Once in a lifetime, gone, just like that."

"You're just saying that because you think the bird is lonely."

"Well, it's the truth," I say.

"Love can always be found again," my mom whispers. "Even if you lose it. You just have to look in the right places."

"Even us?"

She smiles. "All of us." Then she grabs my hand and says, "C'mon. I baked some cookies that are waiting for you." She winks as she pulls me along. "And maybe a scoop of ice cream on top."

A beaming smile forms on my face, and for a moment, I can forget all about the heartaches of this world.

Even if it only lasts for a moment. That moment is one I'll cherish.

***

Present

Why am I doing this again?

Oh right, because I stupidly thought college was a good idea.

It would've been, if the dude I slept with wasn't my fucking professor ... and staring at me every other minute.

Every time he drops a question, bam, he gives me that intense look again. And each time, I blush like hell. I swear I can see him smile when I do. It's like he thinks it's funny. And you know what? I'm embarrassed as fuck, but I can't keep my eyes off him either. That cocky smile just does something to me, makes me remember all the dirty things he did to me. And then I swoon all over ... over a guy I can't have.

God, this is fucked up.

But I can't leave either.

Not again.

That would be even more embarrassing, so I stick it out until the class is over.

I pack up as quickly as I can, trying not to look at him as I get up from my seat.

But then his voice rings through the auditorium. "Oh, Hailey Walters ... I still want to discuss something with you."

I freeze in place as the other students pass me.

"I'll see you later then," Lesley mouths at me before walking out.

I wanted to grab her, but she was too far ahead for me to beg her to stay.

Fuck.

Now, I'm all alone with *him*.

I spin on my heels only to be met with a smug smile and a stare. He's still sitting behind his desk, his hand placed firmly on the wood like he knows he's got me cornered. Damn him.

"C'mon," he says, beckoning me.

I step down the stairs slowly, not taking my eyes off him because I feel like he could just appear in front of me if I did. I stand in front of his desk as he looks up at me with discerning eyes that almost demand attention.

"Why so nervous?"

I swallow. "I'm not nervous."

"I can see you fiddling your fingers." He points, and I look down, then hide my hands behind my back, feeling caught doing something I didn't even know I was doing.

"I just wanted to talk."

"About what?" I ask.

"About us."

The way he says it makes all the hairs on the back of my neck stand up … in a good way.

He leans on his desk and gets up, his chair scooting back inches from the imposing stance. "Let's just get this out of the way, shall we? Do you want this to be awkward?"

"No, not really."

"Me neither." He steps away from his desk, and I instinctively turn to face him as he walks around to me. "Which is why I wanted to talk. I just want to know we're on the same terms."

"Depends on what those terms are," I say, folding my arms.

"The terms being that you are my student and I am your

teacher, and we are to behave accordingly."

"Right." I don't understand where he's going with this.

"We should act professionally," he adds, nodding, as he paces around. He looks up at me as if he's looking for an answer.

"Yes. But—"

He walks toward me, and then past me, circling around like a vulture stalking its prey. "And neither of us will talk about our private time together with anyone else. Agreed?"

"Okay ... but that doesn't mean I'm going to forget."

As he passes me, I swear I can see him narrow his eyes. "Neither will I, Miss Walters. I could never."

Suddenly, I feel a rush of hot air on my neck ... and a quick brush of his finger on my back, tingling all the way down my spine.

***

THOMAS

I don't know why I touched her.

I saw her standing there with her sassy attitude, and all I could think of was putting my hands on her. So I did. It just happened. I couldn't stop myself.

I should have.

But for some reason, I don't want to; even though I know it's wrong.

She's not just the girl I fucked now. She's a student, and I should behave properly. Too bad my mind is so fucking dirty when I'm around her; I'm anything but proper right now.

I can feel her body stiffen from just a stroke of my finger. I know she feels it too … The effect I have on her. How she gets me all riled up just by looking at me. Maybe that's why we keep running into each other. We can't stay away … and maybe that's also why we're fighting it so damn hard.

"I just want to know …" I say. "Will you be missing more classes?"

"What? Um … I don't know," she says, quickly recapturing herself.

"That's not an answer." I place my hand on the desk, close to where she's standing, and I lean in. I can't stop myself. I want to get closer, even though I know I shouldn't. Too bad my dick doesn't listen to my brain.

"Are we done here?" she asks, crossing her arms.

She turns around and starts to walk away from me, and I can't shake that feeling where I just want to grab her and make her stay. Especially when I see that ass of hers swaying from side to side. Makes me want to spank her again.

Fuck. Things are really getting complicated now.

"You'd better show up tomorrow," I say.

She glances at me over her shoulder. "Or else?"

I smirk, thinking of all the dirty things I could do to her.

"You know *exactly* what will happen if you don't." The words roll off my tongue before I realize it, and I know I can't take it back. It's not just a harmless joke. It's a promise.

She just stares at me with this shocked look on her face, and then quickly turns to rush off.

God, this is so fucked up … and I love it all the same.

There's just something about that girl, something

intangible but so clearly visible … the need to feel wanted. I can taste it in the air—her fear of not being seen, not being heard. It's as if she goes through life without really feeling at all. The ghost-like gaze in her eyes tells me there's so much more to her than what she lets people see.

And I can't wait to discover.

Should I?

Fuck, no.

But I wasn't expecting her to show up in my class either.

What's been done can't be changed. We had sex, and I told myself I could forget and move on, just like with all the other girls.

Except she isn't just any girl.

She's a student. *My* student.

And because of her, I might just break the rules …

***

Later that night

The first thing I do when I get home is grab my computer and open Facebook.

It's nothing random. I'm looking at her.

Yesterday was the same.

I searched through all her pictures. Stalked her profile. Checked her posts.

She's a raunchy girl. Likes to drink and party all day long, even when she isn't supposed to. She wears vibrant colors, just like her hair, like she wants to scream to the world and tell us she's here. She shouts a lot and uses more emoji than words. She also likes to show off her piercing, which I think suits her well. I never find her reading a book or taking pictures in class. Neither do I find any posts about her parents or any family for that matter. Or I'm just not looking hard enough.

The more I look at her profile, the more I feel like I'm getting to know her, even though the story is one-sided. Maybe this makes me a pervert, but I think of it differently. At least, I'm doing it in private … and at least, she doesn't know.

A few weeks back, she seemed to have been at a party because I see a video of her chugging a beer and licking ice cream from some guy's belly. Guess she really does love the randomness.

Another video is of her dancing, probably taped by her friend. She looks jacked, but her dancing is so sensual that I'm captivated.

I can't stop watching.

Can't stop being completely entranced by her dancing … and the carelessness she exudes.

Just like me, she's looking for an escape.

I can't help but feel connected.

And completely aroused.

Her moves are so seductive that I reach for my pants and start touching myself.

My dick was already hard.

It was hard back when I talked to her in class.

It's hard when I think of her while I shower.

It's hard when I look at her on Facebook.

And it gets even harder when I realize this is so fucking wrong.

Rubbing myself isn't enough anymore, so I pull down

my zipper and tug my dick out.

Her hungry face is looking straight at the camera, and I can almost feel her eyes bore into me.

My cock pulses with need at the sight of her curvy body in that tight red dress she's wearing, and I want to cover her with my load. Dirty images of her flash through my mind.

Her, bent over my desk, ass red from my hand, my cock deep inside her pussy.

Her, sucking my cock until I come inside her mouth, then licking my juices off my cock under the shower.

Her, spreading her legs for me to enjoy, then pounding her until she comes.

Her, tied to my bed, her ass up and ready for the taking.

I want her.

I want her so badly ... that I come from the thought alone.

I moan out loud as my cum shoots all over my pants, the desk, my wall.

Fuck.

I needed that badly too.

Damn, that girl has driven me crazy with need.

I sigh. Look at this mess. Now, I'm gonna have to clean it up.

But I can't help but think that one day I'm going to make her clean it all up with just her tongue.

And that day may come sooner than I thought.

See, this is why I don't return for seconds ... because I can't let them go.

It's not good for her or for me.

Especially considering she's my student.

Fuck me.

My phone suddenly rings, and I check the number.

Fuck, just who I needed.

I don't pick up. Instead, I get up and grab a few tissues to clean myself and the mess I've made all over my desk. But as I throw away the tissues, the phone rings again, making me sigh.

She really isn't giving up, is she?

Guess my further investigation of Hailey's profile will have to wait.

Chapter 6

Hailey

"Look," Lesley says. "I can make dicks with my smoke."

She takes a drag of her cigarette and blows out the air in a bigger circle and then a smaller stream, which sort of looks like a dick ... but not really.

"Looks more like a droopy sock to me."

"Oh, fuck you. Can you do it better?"

"No, and I'm not even trying," I say. "All I can blow is fucking pussies."

"How?" she muses.

I take a drag and blow out a ring. "See? Hole."

Lesley laughs. "That's one big-ass pussy. That would fit like five dicks."

"Six now. It keeps growing bigger."

We both laugh out loud as we lean against the school building, watching the oncoming traffic from afar. I like standing out here, just watching people like it's my job. Beats sitting in class listening to a lecture. I guess I'm more of a people watcher than an actual participant in 'real-life.' Whatever the fuck that is.

"Oh, my …" Lesley suddenly says. "Look!"

She points at a car in the parking lot, and I watch as Mr. Hard steps out of the passenger's side. He walks to the driver's side and waits until the window rolls down. It's a woman, and she smiles coyly as he sticks his head through the window. I can't see what they're doing, but I know enough. It can't be good.

"Uh-oh … looks like Mr. Hard-ass is taken," Lesley jests.

I bite my tongue.

Then I see him turn around and pace toward us.

"Fuck, turn around." I shove her aside. "That way."

"Whoa, what are you doing?"

"I really don't wanna talk with a professor right now. It's already awkward enough in class," I say.

"Okay, okay."

We walk to the back of the building and wait. I peek around the corner right when he enters the building. I sigh to myself when he's out of my sight. If she's right … fuck. I hate to think about it, so I shut it out. I throw my cigarette on the ground and stomp it out.

"I'm really not feeling class today," I say.

"What? You wanna skip? Again?"

"Yeah, why not?" I shrug. "Not like we'll miss anything. All the classes are recorded and can be watched online."

"Yeah, but he'll probably give extra homework that you won't get if you're not there."

I smirk as I turn around while walking backward. "Isn't that the point?"

She frowns. "Okay … you do realize you need to pass a test soon?"

"I know." I shrug. "But not right now."

She still stands there, even though I'm walking farther away. "C'mon," I yell.

"No, I think I'll go to class today," she says.

"Aww …" I make a pouty face.

"You do what you want, okay?" she yells back. "I'll see you later."

"Fine. Be a party pooper!"

She puts her middle finger in the air, so I throw up two. We both smile and then I turn around and go the other way. I don't know where I'm going, and I don't care. I just want to get away.

Run. Run. Run. That's all I've ever done.

***

Three years ago

Every time I enter my house, it feels like I stepped into a funeral without knowing someone died.

The closed curtains block the sunlight, with only the light of the lamp in the kitchen lighting the house. It smells of burning cigarettes and alcohol, mixed with a hint of spices.

I find my mother in the kitchen, putting her blood,

sweat, and tears into creating the perfect tomato soup.

"Hi," I say quickly, trying not to interrupt her, but she still looks my way.

The big bruise on her face makes me stop in my tracks. "Hi, honey! Where've you been?"

"Just hanging with friends," I say, tucking my hair behind my ears because I don't know what else to do when I see the black mark on her face.

I make everything I do sound as casual as possible, so I don't draw attention to the fact that I'd do pretty much anything, even if it's boring as fuck, just to stay away from home.

She smiles awkwardly, only to cover up her bruise with a bit of her hair.

We're both in denial.

Suddenly, the front door slams open, inviting in the dark air of rage.

"I'm gonna go to my room," I say without looking back.

"Margaret! I'm hungry!"

His voice alone makes me speed walk.

I only just manage to slam my door shut before he explodes.

"Fuck! Why'd you make this crap? You know I always fucking want chicken soup!" I hear him yell.

"I thought I'd make something different today … to surprise you," my mom says with her soft voice.

"I hate tomato soup!"

I hear something metallic clatter on the floor, and I just know it's the pan.

"Look what you made me do!" His voice is louder than anything I've heard before.

So loud, it makes me want to scream.

"Clean it up and make something else before I throw you and your filthy rat outta this house!" he yells.

Tears fill my eyes, but I don't want them now.

I feel so helpless.

I wish I could go to my mom and fight for her, even when she refuses to fight back.

I would hit him if I knew I had the strength to match his.

In a haze, I grab my iPod and earplugs and put them in. They don't drown out the noise until I turn on the music. "Teen Idle" by Marina and the Diamonds blares through.

Loud, so it drowns out their fighting.

Louder, so I don't have to hear her cries.

So loud, my ears almost feel like they're going to burst, but I don't care.

This music is the only thing I have.

It makes me feel alive in a world that died a slow, miserable death.

***

THOMAS

Now

One empty seat.

Hers.

Does she think she can play around with me?

When I say she needs to be there, I mean it.

I give my class an assignment to focus on so I can get to

work in peace. I open my laptop and type in her name on Facebook. Luckily, I don't need to friend her to be able to private message her.

Thomas: Where are you?

It takes her a while to answer, and I tap my fingers on the desk, annoyed at the fact that she defied my rules.

Thomas: Answer me.

Hailey: Nowhere.

Thomas: Nowhere in class, that's right.

Hailey: Since when are you on Facebook?

Thomas: Since I met you.

I'm not afraid to admit I've been watching her. I know it's against the rules, but I already broke them, so being careful now isn't of much use. I just want her to be here. I don't care what I have to do to make it happen.

Hailey: Stalker, much?

Thomas: Maybe if you got your ass back into class, I wouldn't have to.

Hailey: Sorry, but I'm really not feeling up to it right now.

Thomas: Are you sick?

Hailey: I've been sick all morning. I never left bed.

Thomas: Really now? Because I could have swore I saw you standing near the school door this morning.

It takes her a while to answer, so I guess she didn't expect me to know she wasn't actually sick. I see right through bullshit. Students try that all the time, but it isn't going to work on me. Especially not when *she* tries it.

Hailey: Fine. Yes, I was there. Now, I'm not. Just leave me alone.

Thomas: No. You will come to school. Now.

Hailey: Why do you care so much? Got a crush on me or something?

Thomas: Don't test my patience, Hailey.

She's pushing me to my limit, but I won't let her go over it. If she won't listen to me, I'll teach her to listen … my way.

Hailey: Isn't this like 'strictly forbidden' or something?

Thomas: Oh, we've already gone way past the forbidden line … You know, I'm curious. Tell me who you're running from? Because it's obviously not just me.

Hailey: I'm not running from anyone, and certainly not you.

Thomas: Good. Then you can come to class like you're supposed to.

It takes her a while to respond. She must be feeling pressured. Good. She should learn to listen sometimes. It's in her best interest to go to class … and to be near me. I could teach her a few things no one else can.

Hailey: I wouldn't tell you, even if I were.

Thomas: I know. And you don't have to tell me, just as long as you get to class right now.

Hailey: Or else?

Thomas: Oh … you don't even know what I'm capable of, but I think you get the picture. Now … Come. Here.

She stops replying to my messages, so I guess she turned off her phone. Pity.
If she doesn't materialize within ten minutes, I don't think I'll be able to contain myself. I can't believe she skipped class again.
What is she thinking? Just because we fucked does not mean she can jeopardize her schoolwork. I won't let her do that. That would look bad for me too, since I'm the one

who fucked her.

I close my laptop and pick up a pencil, watching the class work. I don't interrupt them, as I have far more important things on my mind. Like how I'm going to make her pay for skipping class again. What would be a fitting punishment?

Extra homework, so she can catch up?

A lecture in front of the whole class so she won't screw up again?

Or should I just wait until we're alone, then bend her over my desk and spank her ass until it's red?

I put my pencil in my mouth and start biting, as I need something to calm myself down before I get a boner. God, right in front of these students.

It's so wrong, but I can't stop thinking about it either.

When she's in front of me, I can see straight through her clothes. Her naked body is still so vivid and in the forefront of my mind … it's like I can't even think about anything else anymore.

All I want is to fuck her again.

And then tell her how stupid she is for wasting her time in college like this.

I wonder why she's doing this. It can't be just because of me … or maybe it is.

But I don't want to give myself that much credit. After all, I was just a way for her to get rid of her virgin status.

There must be more going on in her life that makes her so careless. I should've known. When a girl like her fucks a man like me, it isn't just random. There's always more to it. Just like there is to me.

When class is over, I spit out my pencil and tap the

table. "That's it, guys! Time to pack up. See you Monday."

The students pack their things, get up, and leave, while I sit here and stare ahead. The clock ticks on and on, and nothing happens. I enjoy the silence, as long as it lasts.

When the door creaks open, I'm all ears.

Chapter 7

Hailey

When I open the door and peek inside, the seats are completely empty. Fuck. I'm too late.

"Come in."

My ears perk up at the sound of his voice, and I push the door open farther.

Thomas spins his chair around and greets me with a warm, seductive smile. "Hailey. How nice of you to come."

He puts so much emphasis on that last word that it makes me quiver in place.

I swallow away the nerves and walk inside.

He picks up a pencil and starts to play with it, casually flipping it between two fingers, his eyes completely focused on me. I struggle not to blush from his blatant stare as I stand in front of his desk, waiting for him to tell me how I broke the rules.

"So … you're finally here," he muses, as if he wants to rub it in.

I cock my head and take a deep breath, but I don't respond.

"What made you come?"

Again, that emphasis … it's as if he wants me to think about other dirtier things. "You told me to come."

"Yes. Where you should've been for about an hour or two. Class is over now. You missed it."

"Guess so. Sorry." I shrug.

"No, you're not," he says, narrowing his eyes. "And still, you came back. Why?"

I rub my lips together. "I don't know."

"You … *wanted* to come back."

"Not really."

"Yes, you did. Otherwise, you wouldn't have. The power of persuasion." He smirks. "You came back because *I* told you to." He leans back in his chair, one leg over the other.

"I came back because I know I should've been here."

"But you only came back after I told you to. You felt like you needed to listen to me."

I frown. "Where are you going with this?"

He smiles and then scoots back his chair and gets up. "Nowhere."

God, he's playing me. Again.

"Okay, just give it to me straight," I say.

"Oh, I will …" he muses, placing the pencil on the desk.

"What do you want from me? No games."

"I'm not playing games. If I were, you'd know." He circles around his desk, inching closer to me.

I don't even dare blink; afraid he'll be right behind me and pounce me on the desk.

I'm not afraid of him or what he can do. I'm afraid of my own resistance because I have none when it comes to him.

"You skipped class today. Again," he says. "I told you not to do that. So why did you? Do you like getting under my skin?"

He paces behind me while I keep staring ahead, not wanting to look at him ... Because every time I do, I feel weak in the knees.

"Do you dislike my classes? Think you can't learn anything? Or are you just not interested?"

"None of those."

"Then what?"

It's almost as if he's genuinely curious. Like he really cares what I think.

But why would he ... he's my professor, and I'm his student. That's all, right?

Because he said that's all we were ... or all we should be.

And professors don't care about their student's interest the way he cares about mine.

I'm almost inclined to answer him, but when I think back to this morning, I remember the car and the woman who drove him to work. I can't help but wonder ...

"This morning ... I saw you step out of a car. A woman was driving."

"Oh ..." He smiles briefly as I turn my head. "So that's what this is all about."

I don't say a word. I'm not going to reveal my feelings to him.

Suddenly, I feel his fingers on my neck again, and his lips are so close to my ear I stop breathing for a second. "You're jealous."

"I'm not," I retort.

"It's okay ... You don't have to worry about her," he whispers in my ear.

His fingers snake down my neck, my shoulders, and my entire back, leaving goose bumps everywhere until they rest on my waist. His body towers behind me, and I can't help but lean back into his grasp as he holds me.

"But you broke my rules, Hailey. You didn't come to class, even when I told you to. Do you understand what that means?"

I nod slowly. Not because I know what it means, but because I *want* to know.

"I'm going to teach you my rules," he whispers, and his tongue briefly darts out to lick my earlobe, sending waves of heat down my body.

Then he steps back, leaving the air thick with desire.

Before I can glance over my shoulder, his commanding voice takes over.

"Bend over."

I hesitate.

Three seconds.

That's all it takes for me to actually go through with it.

My body leans over on its own while my brain shouts at me. What am I doing? Why am I doing this?

"Lower. Facedown on the desk."

I don't know why, but I listen.

With my head and tits on the desk, I suck in a breath, awaiting the next move.

I'm insane. Lost my fucking mind.

His hand gently pets my back, gliding down until he's on my ass ... where he grasps me firmly, squeezing tight. I hiss, biting my lip. Memories of our night together resurface, my panties getting wet with just his touch.

"You tempt me too much, Hailey ..." he murmurs with a deliciously low voice.

His hand skims down my skirt and roughly shoves it up, pulling it over my back.

I freeze.

What the fuck.

What the fuck, what the fuck, what the fuck?

I shiver as his hand travels over my panties and across my ass, and my heart beat shoots through the roof. This is crazy. We're in a room that can't be locked. Anyone could come in at any time. Anyone could see us.

And still, I don't stop him.

I don't say no.

And I don't want to.

But then his hand comes down on my ass.

Hard.

"You make me do bad ... bad things, Hailey."

Again.

I slam my lips together to prevent any sound from spilling out.

His hand is rough and ruthless as it spanks my ass again and again.

One after the other until both my cheeks zing with red-hot pain.

My body bucks against the table each time his hand strikes my ass. It hurts, but not enough to make me cry. Enough to make my legs shake with desire, though.

It's sick, completely twisted, yet I still don't want to tell him to stop.

Maybe I just don't want to give him the satisfaction of winning our argument. Or maybe I'm willing to take whatever he's willing to give.

"You have such a nice ass …" he says softly, rubbing my painful ass with his flat hand. Every movement makes me twitch with excitement. "It should be cherished. Especially when red. Has anyone ever told you that before?"

I shake my head.

He fists my hair and pulls my head back enough for me to gasp. "Answer when I ask you a question."

"No," I say.

"It's Sir for you, Hailey." He grabs my ass again, this time even harder than before. "Say it again."

"No, Sir."

I moan out loud when he smacks me again.

"Good girl." I can almost hear the smile in his voice.

I expect him to spank me some more, but his fingers are so gentle on my skin that it makes me relax. My muscles unwind from all the tension, but my pussy is thumping so hard I can feel it through my entire body.

When his hand disappears, I'm left struggling to breathe.

After a while, I look back over my shoulder.

He's not even there anymore. He's standing at another table, gathering pieces of paper and putting them in a stack.

Confused, I stand up again and pull my skirt back down. He doesn't look at me, which surprises me, after what he just did.

Jesus Christ.

I can't even think about it straight.

What just happened here?

I step back slowly, trying not to make a sound. As I turn, my eyes search the room, hoping I don't find anyone who has been sneaking a peek. Luckily, I don't see anything but a door, to which I immediately start to walk.

Right before I open the door, his voice booms once more through the room, reminding me who's in charge. "I'll see you Monday, Hailey. Don't be late."

Chapter 8

Hailey

"Cheers!" Lesley taps my cup with hers and then sips on her drink.

I smile at her but don't immediately drink.

Normally, I wouldn't hesitate to chug the alcohol, but I'm really not in the mood right now. The party is fine. Actually, it's amazing. Lots of lights, loud music, people shouting and singing along. The mood is perfect, and on a Sunday night, I couldn't ask for anything more.

But I've been feeling awkward in my own skin ever since that meeting with Thomas. No matter what I do, I can't get into it. Whether it's partying, going someplace, or even talking with Lesley. Nothing can take my mind off him, which makes me confused.

I shouldn't be having these thoughts, let alone these feelings.

But fuck me … did it feel right when he had his hands all over me.

Am I supposed to want my professor?

Fuck, no.

And he's definitely not supposed to spank his student.

So many things are wrong with this, on so many different levels, and still, I can't stop thinking about it. Even now, it makes me blush. I don't blush. Ever.

Fuck me. I've really lost it this time.

"You okay?" Lesley asks, pulling me from my thoughts.

"Yeah, I'm fine. Just thinking about tomorrow."

"What's tomorrow when you have today?" She bites her lip as she grabs my hand and pulls me back into the crowd. "C'mon, let's dance."

"I haven't finished my drink," I say, quickly taking a sip.

"Drink it while we dance, I don't care. Just have fun and enjoy yourself. You obviously need it. You've been so tense lately."

"Tell me about it," I say, taking another sip as we walk to the middle of the dance floor.

"Something's up with you," she says. "You're still hiding shit, aren't you?"

I shrug and shake my head. "Nah. You're delusional."

"Right." She smiles. "I'm gonna pull it out of you one day. Just wait."

"Sure, you will," I say, taking the last sip. "But first … let's party!" I shout out loud, and the crowd goes along, then I throw my cup in the air and spin.

Like two crazy chicks, we dance, not giving a shit what

anyone thinks of our wacky moves. I'm just doing my thing, shaking my hips, bobbing to the beat, and enjoying the music. I'm drifting away into my own wonderland where everything is perfect and tomorrow is a long way to go. I don't wanna be anywhere but here—far, far away from reality and the homework I was supposed to do.

But somehow, that single thought pulls me right back into the moment. In my head, I still hear his voice, pushing me not to disappoint him.

Goddammit.

"Hey, I'm gonna grab another drink. Want one too?" Lesley asks.

"Nah, I'm good."

She leaves and I continue to sway my hips in the air, not giving a shit who's watching. Some dude dances beside me, and I don't mind, as long as he doesn't touch me. I'm game for talking, but no personal details, only fun things. If they ask me for a name, I don't give them any. They call me the redhead or 'that girl with the nose piercing,' which is fine by me.

As long as they don't get too close, I'm good.

After a while, I start to wonder where Lesley's at. She's probably getting smashed somewhere. I should probably stop her because she's bad when it comes to alcohol. Pretty much the same as I am. We drink until we're laughing our asses off, and then we go home.

Except I can't fucking see her anywhere. Frowning, I search for her until I find her near the minibar, taking a beer from a dude I don't even recognize, let alone know.

I make my way over there, watching her from afar. They're talking, but another guy steps in and holds out his phone to her. She laughs as he shows her something, but there's no smile on my face. The dude who handed her the beer casually hovers his fingers over the tip of the bottle.

I hurry my pace when I see her bring the bottle to her lips.

"Les, don't!" I yell, but it's already too late. She's already drunk the beer and the guys beside her disappear into the crowds. Fuck.

"What's wrong with—" Lesley shouts back as I rip the bottle away from her hand.

"It's spiked."

Her eyes widen. "What?"

"C'mon, we're outta here." I grab her hand and pull her with me through the room, carefully checking for anyone who will stop us. I know why they gave this to her, and I'm not letting them get their hands on her again. I'd fucking kill them myself if they ever touch her.

"Oh, god …" she mumbles, and she stumbles behind me.

I barely manage to hold her up. "Don't fall," I say. "Let's get home quickly."

"I don't feel so good."

"I know, but you gotta hold on." I put my arm under her shoulder and pull her with me, eyeing the boys in the room. One of them gazes straight back at me, and I just know it was him. I can tell from the way he looks, and for a second, I actually contemplate going over to him and smacking the ever-living shit out of him. However, I can't leave her alone, not even for a minute, so I give him a big middle finger from across the room and drag Lesley out.

"Whe-ere are w-we going?" Lesley stutters, her face

droopy.

"Home," I say, pulling her across the parking lot.

"Home where?"

"Our dorm."

"Oh … right." She giggles out loud.

"You're smashed," I say as I bring her to a bench. "Sit down."

"Why?"

"Because I need to call a cab."

"Can't you drive?"

"We didn't come here in my car; we came here in a cab."

"Oh, shit. I forgot." She laughs again. "Sorry."

"I know; it's not your fault." I sigh while I dial the number.

When I'm done ordering the cab, I sit down beside her and put my hand on her forehead. "You're heating up."

She puts her head on my shoulder. "I feel like I need to puke."

"If you do, don't throw up on me. Lean that way." I point at the bush next to her.

"I don't know. Maybe I can keep it together. At least 'til we're home."

I pat her back and take a deep breath, trying to calm myself.

I'm fuming. How could that motherfucker drug her? And why did she let it happen? She should've known better.

"I'm sorry, Hailey," she mutters out of nowhere.

"Shh …" I say, rubbing her. "It's okay. I'm just glad I got you outta there before they got their hands on you."

"I feel so dizzy. I just know it's something bad. GHB

maybe."

I nod. "Want me to call a doctor too?"

"Nah ... I just wanna sleep it off." She yawns. "I'm so fucking tired all the sudden."

"That's the drugs. You were still dancing only minutes ago."

"Fuckers. I should've known this would happen. That party was too good to be true."

"I know, lots of older guys too. And too much booze, it was suspicious."

"Exactly." She tries to fist bump me but fails, laughing again. "Thanks"—she looks up at me—"for always having my back."

"Of course. That's what friends are for, right?"

"To stop you from drinking booze." She puts her arm around me and hugs me. "To stop me from getting pounded in a van by a guy I don't even know. Or worse."

I don't say anything. I just grab her hand and hold her tight because that's the only right thing to do.

"You're squashing me with your boobs," she says, coughing.

I laugh and release her. "Sorry."

She turns her head toward me and gloats like a shithead. "The force is strong with these."

"Strong, the alcohol smells." I snigger.

"Shut up, Yoda."

I shrug. "Started it, you did."

"Hailey ... I am your father."

I shove her aside. "Stop."

She giggles. "Stop, I cannot."

"Nerd."

"Says the girl with the red hair and rainbow colored panties." She laughs at me so hard, she struggles to breathe.

"I haven't worn those in years!" I say.

"Can't. Forget." She almost dies from laughter, I swear.

"Yeah, you're laughing now. But if you ever fall asleep again, I'm so going to put them on your ass."

"You wouldn't." She narrows her eyes at me.

"Oh, I dare …"

I fucking dare so hard, I think I'm going to do it tonight when she least expects it.

And then draw a fucking dick on her face too, for good measure.

***

The next morning

I wake up with the salt stuck to my eyes, but I can clearly see the sun shining brightly through the windows. That's weird … there's usually not that much sunlight when I wake up for school.

School.

Fuck.

I shoot up from my bed and grab my alarm clock. Which I forgot to set.

"Fuck!" I yell.

"Hnmmmggrrr." Lesley's moan makes me turn my head, which I shouldn't have done because there's a bucket filled with puke next to her bed.

"Aw, gross," I mutter as I jump out of bed.

"What are you doing?" she grumbles.

"I have class," I say, scrambling to gather my clothes off the floor, which is also when I notice I'm still wearing yesterday's clothes. Apparently, I never took off my red dress and jumped straight into bed with it.

I guess taking care of Lesley really did a number on me.

I had to hold her hair half the night while she filled the toilet bowl.

It wasn't a pretty sight, and I don't wanna remember. It took up so many hours of my night. I'm just glad we were lucky enough to score a private bathroom so no one else had to witness that. When I finally got her to bed and crawled into my own, I must've forgotten to set the alarm.

Fuck.

I completely forgot it was school day too.

Putting on my clothes in a hurry, I forget to do my hair, leaving my make-up as butchered as it was. One sock is purple, the other green. I couldn't find any others, so this'll have to do. I throw everything I have in my bag, probably forgetting a few things.

"Where you going?" Lesley asks.

"You just asked that. God, never mind. Just stay in bed. Sleep," I grumble. She's not fit for class today, so best just let her sleep this one off.

"Okay …" she mumbles, too tired to even realize what's going on.

Before I rush out the door, I pull on the curtains so the sun won't keep her up. Too bad I was too tired to actually put my rainbow underwear on her ass and draw a dick on her face. Oh, well.

As I rush out the door, I check the clock. I'm so fucking late; it's not even classy to show up anymore.

But I will.

I *will* fucking be there because … I don't know why.

I just know I have to be there.

It's *his* class, after all.

Who knows what will happen if I don't show up.

The thought should scare me, but it doesn't. It excites me.

Makes me anxious to see what's in store for me, even though this time I actually have good reasons for why I was absent. He'll probably still be mad, though.

Damn.

I don't even know why I care so much. Should I? Is it wrong if I do?

The guy just has an effect on me like no one else.

It's like he makes me do things I didn't think I would ever do for anyone. Yet I'd do them for him just because he tells me to.

When I'm finally there, I'm panting from running, and when I check the clock, I still didn't make it in time. Before I go in, I swallow away the lump in my throat and then peek around the corner. Again, it's empty, and my courage sinks into my shoes.

I really fucking messed up.

I already missed three classes. It's like I'm doomed to fail.

"Come in."

Fuck.

Just his voice alone gives me the shivers.

I gather what's left of my courage and step inside with my head held high.

I know why I'm late. I have a good reason. Still, it's no

excuse.

His eyes are like those of a hawk zooming in on its prey as I step down into his territory. Every time I look at him, my body radiates with heat. I can still feel his hand scorching on my skin, my ass red with his mark.

It felt so wrong ...

But so right too.

I walk toward him as he sits behind his desk with an arrogant smile on his face. He casually leans to the side as I stop in front of him and drop my bag.

"You. Weren't. Here."

He doesn't seem happy. At all.

I suck my bottom lip. "I know."

His eyes narrow.

And I do the only thing I can think of.

I lower my head, bend over, and say, "Punish me."

Chapter 9

THOMAS

She wants me to punish her.

Want.

She *wants* me.

Spanking her was my dirty dream.

The dirty sin I committed when she stepped into my classroom.

The moment I put my hands on her, I knew it was wrong, but I couldn't stop myself.

When I finally managed to control myself and turned my back on her, she left so quickly …

I thought I'd fucked up.

With my desires out of control, I thought I'd pushed her past her limit.

And now, she comes here, begging for more?

My jaw almost drops, but I manage to compose myself and stand up from my seat.

I don't say a word.

All my mouth wants to do right now is kiss her. It doesn't want to talk.

But that's not what she came here for.

She knew she had class and that she was late again, and still, she dared to step foot in my classroom.

She's insane. Or maybe she's looking for that extra stimulation. Stimulation I'm more than willing to give.

I step toward her, carefully walking around the desk, watching her. But she doesn't move from her spot. It's as if she's determined for me to spank her again. Like she knows this is the only way to amend her mistake, even if it's so fucking wrong …

It's what I want. What I need. What I crave.

And what she needs as well.

As I stand behind her, I can't help admire her ass. Every time I look at it, it's as if I've never seen it before; that's how precious it is. Especially when she bends over my desk and begs me to spank her like that.

"Do you know what you're asking from me?"

She nods. "Yes."

I grin and bite my bottom lip. "I hope you know I'll enjoy this thoroughly."

I grab her zipper, pull it down, and pop her button, ripping both her jeans and panties down in one go. She doesn't even flinch when I put my hands on her naked skin and rub her. Her ass is so cold … it could use a warm-up.

SMACK!

My slap reverberates through the entire room, the sound music to my ears.

Another one to the other cheek and her body bounces against the table.

The third slap has her on her tiptoes.

I place my hand on her back and say, "Stay still."

She sucks in a ragged breath as I softly caress her ass.

Then I spank her again.

Each hit a little harder than the one before.

I continue until both her ass cheeks are red and her skin glows with my print. Such a fine sight.

When I've spanked her for the final time, her body is quivering, and my cock is tenting against my pants.

My eyes glide over her naked ass and the rest of her body, lingering on her face which lies flat on my desk.

Fucking hell.

It's too much.

My hands instinctively move to my crotch, pulling down my zipper without a second thought. I take out my eager cock and start rubbing it. With one hand, I caress her sweet, red ass while I work myself with the other. I can't stop myself, even if I wanted to, which I don't.

I feel possessed.

Consumed by the thought of coming all over her ass marked with my handprint.

She lies on the table without making a sound, her breathing slow and steady as I slide my fingers across her ass and between her slit. She shivers a little as I almost reach her pussy, but then pull back my fingers to continue touching her ass.

The silence between us is deafening, but to me, it only

adds to the pleasure as I can hear my own hand flicking over the tip of my cock. Pre-cum serves as the lube, which I spread all over my shaft as I increase my speed. Moans escape my mouth as I hover above her red ass and clamp it tight.

With my fingers digging into her skin, I groan and come.

Cum shoots onto her ass, dripping along her slit as I pour my load on her.

God, the release feels so good ... so wrong too, but fuck, so good.

When I'm done, I swipe my cock along her skin before putting it back into my pants.

I reach for her pants and pull them up, covering her naked, cum-painted ass with her panties again.

She gasps. "What are—"

"Giving you what you deserve."

Her cheeks flush red. Almost the same shade as her ass is right now.

I close her button and zip her up again. "You'll wear this the rest of the day."

"What? Why?" she asks, turning around.

"Because I say so," I say with a smirk.

"But it has your cum all over it."

I place a finger on her lips. "Shhh ..."

She scowls. "You can't expect me—"

"I expect you to stay here and shut up." I give her a brash smile and then walk over to one of the tables to grab a chair, which I bring to my desk. "Sit."

I cock my head and point at it with my eyes until she gets the message.

She makes a face as her ass touches the hard wood but

then repositions herself, her lips pursed as if she refuses to acknowledge the fact that A. her ass hurts, and B. she'll have to feel my juices all day long.

I can't help but smile at the thought.

Walking to the other end of the desk, I try to banish the dirty thoughts from my head. I spanked her and then jerked myself off all over her, staining her panties with my cum. It felt fucking wonderful, but now, I feel bad. Bad for letting her tempt me again.

It shouldn't have happened, so I'll just pretend it never did.

I sit down across from her and reach for the papers on my desk.

"Um … what are you doing?" she asks.

"Grabbing your homework."

"Homework?" Her voice sounds like she doesn't understand why I'd ever make her do that. As if I'm not still her teacher and this is not a classroom.

"Yes, homework," I repeat, placing a sheet of questions in front of her. "Which you'll do right here in front of me."

"Why?"

"Isn't it obvious?" I raise a brow. "You missed class. Now, you catch up."

She makes a face. "You can't be serious."

I frown right back. "Do I look like I'm joking?"

She sighs, sits back, and crosses her arms. "No. I don't understand you."

"There's not so much to understand, Hailey. I'm your teacher, and you're my student, so that means you'll do homework when I ask you to, and you'll get extra lessons if you skip."

"And why would I do that?" she asks.

I smile at her, leaning over the desk. "Because I want you to."

We engage in a stare down. After a while, she sits up again and looks at the sheet of paper. "Can't."

"Why not?" I ask.

"No pen." She shrugs, a cheeky smile on her face.

"I can help you with that." I reach into my drawer and take out a pen, placing it on top of the sheet. "Now, you can."

She sighs out loud again, staring at the paper.

Then she looks at me again. I don't budge. Neither does she.

"Can I at least go to the bathroom first?"

"No," I say, with a stern voice.

She frowns. After another sigh, she picks up the pen and puts it on the paper. A bit of muttering comes from her mouth, but I can't hear it, so I say, "Sorry, what was that?"

"Nothing," she says, circling an answer.

"Say it again," I say.

She briefly glances up at me and narrows her eyes. "I said you're a fucking dick." A tiny smile is added. "Should've accepted the 'nothing' when you had the chance."

"And maybe you should have accepted that you need to come to class like I tell you to so this won't have to happen." I smile back at her.

She raises one brow but then returns her attention to the questions on the paper.

"So ... now that I've punished you for being late and not showing up again ... explain to me why you weren't here."

She mulls it over a bit before answering. "I overslept, but I had a good reason. My friend, Lesley … she got into some trouble at a party. She was drugged, and I had to take her home. She was sick all night, and I barely slept."

"Oh …"

Fuck. Why didn't she tell me sooner? She actually has a legitimate reason to be late for once. She didn't deserve that spanking. And to have my cum between her ass cheeks. Okay, maybe that last part isn't as much of a punishment as it was an indulgence to me.

"You should've told me," I say. "Then I wouldn't have—"

Her eyes suddenly turn resolute. "I asked for it."

I frown and narrow my eyes. "You're a peculiar one …"

"Thanks, I guess," she says, penning down another answer.

She wobbles a bit in her chair as she bites her lip.

"Painful?" I ask.

"What?" She looks up.

I cock my head. "Your ass."

"Yeah …"

"Good. Next time you won't be late."

I smirk when her eyes dilate.

"I thought you said—"

"No talking. Just finish your homework."

"If I do this," she says, pointing at the paper, "can I go home then?"

I nod. "But …" I lean in and gaze at her with half-mast eyes. "You can't leave until I'm pleased. *Very* pleased."

Chapter 10

THOMAS

Messing with her could get me in trouble. Big trouble. Like kill-my-career trouble, but honestly, I'm not sure if I care anymore.

I tried.

I really fucking tried to keep up the charade.

To put effort into disguising who I really am and what I love.

But I can't do it anymore. Not with her around to push my every goddamn button.

I'm a sucker for a willing woman who can challenge me, and she's exactly the type to tempt me.

I know I'm using her for my own gain, and it's bad.

It's fucking bad.

But at least now I can provide her some extra guidance

she wouldn't otherwise have. Extra tutoring, homework, and help after class ... in whatever way I deem needed.

I mean I do whatever necessary to get my point across.

In this case, spanking her means she'll finally understand that I don't tolerate her tardiness.

Except she really does need to learn to speak up and tell me what's going on so I can adjust. Things like her friend getting sick and Hailey taking care of her are important details for me to know so I don't punish her when she's done something good.

I run my fingers through my hair as I shift positions in my bed. God, I really can't stop thinking about her. It's getting worse and worse by the day. Not that that's a bad thing. At least she can take my mind off other things ...

Things that I push away the moment they even try to get to the forefront of my mind.

At the moment, besides my job, Hailey is pretty much the only bright spot in my life, which says a lot. She seems to kill the pain like nothing else.

I stare at the bottle of painkillers on my nightstand and hesitate to take one.

It would make it easier to sleep.

But I don't want to. I don't want to keep relying on those pills to bring myself into a state of happiness. Or sleep. But I know what *can*.

Thinking of her.

She's been all over my dreams lately, and not just that. Every night, I catch myself scrolling through the photos on her profile just to get a little closer. Maybe that makes me a stalker, but I don't care.

So I reach for my cell phone and start looking, just as I

do every day.

It makes me smile.

Her face makes me feel warm and wanted.

Her body makes me hard and greedy.

Without thinking, I reach for the message button and start to type.

Thomas: Wear something nice to class tomorrow.

Hailey: Xcuse me, but Y are U PMing me on Facebook?

Thomas: Because I can. And stop using that awful text language. You know how to write.

Hailey: Geez. Grumpy? Need another jerk off?

Thomas: I need you to behave, or I *will* jerk off on your ass again. Now, are you going to wear something nice tomorrow or not?

Hailey: Nice? Like pink socks and unicorn shirt nice, or Japanese-schoolgirl-outfit nice?

Thomas: You know what I mean.

Hailey: Okay ... I see where this is going. But why?

Thomas: Don't ask questions you already know the answers to. I'll see you tomorrow.

Hailey: Or else?

Thomas: Don't test my patience.

Hailey: Sorry, can't help it. I'm a rebel.

Thomas: If you don't stop teasing, I'll spank you again.

Hailey: Is that a threat or a promise?

Thomas: Good night, Hailey.

Hailey: I wanna know what I'm doing it for.

Thomas: Go to sleep.

I turn off my phone and place it on the nightstand.
If she replies again, she's in trouble tomorrow. Big time. But I suspect she won't.
After all, she's finally learned what happens when you don't listen to the teacher …

***

Hailey

The next day

It's ridiculous.
I look ridiculous.

Why? Because I'm wearing a fucking miniskirt with actual pantyhose and high heels, coupled with a crop top. I look like a certified hooker. Like I could go out onto the streets right now and get money thrown at my face.

Actually, that's a good thing. I like money.

Although I wouldn't sell my body for it, I'd sure let them throw it at me if they wanted.

Hot damn, I really look nice … and so totally not like me.

This isn't an appropriate school outfit anyway, but who cares?

I don't, that's for sure.

If people are gonna stare, so be it.

He asked me to do this, so I will.

Yes, I'm doing this *for* him.

Yes, I *have* lost my mind.

I mean, after what he did—squirting his cum all over my panties and making me wear them the entire fucking day—I should've been pissed off beyond control. But I wasn't. Well, at first I was royally pissed, but when I first sat down and felt his warmth flow between my slit, I felt so turned on.

I couldn't stop thinking about him. All day long. All I could think about was his cum and how I could feel its slickness mingling with my own.

I just knew that was his intention from the start.

Getting me to fantasize about him … that's just his thing.

And now this.

Dressing up like some doll.

I don't even know why I enjoy it, but I do.

I like being naughty and wrong.

"Wow, you look ..." Lesley says as she walks by. "Different."

"Different good? Or different horrible?" I ask, turning around.

"Neither. No comment." She slams her lips together, but her eyes are still judging me.

"Oh, c'mon. Tell me what you really think."

"Nuh-uh." She shakes her head. "You do you."

"No, I wanna hear it. Give it to me straight."

"I don't wanna be a bitch."

"How is that different from any other day?" I muse, raising a brow.

She rolls her eyes. "Oh, fuck you. Okay, fine, you look like a hooker. Happy now?"

"Yes." I grin.

"Why is that a good thing?" she asks as I grab my backpack.

"Because that's exactly what I was aiming for."

"Are you looking for a job on the side or something? Jesus, Hailey, I know you had fun on your first time, but I wouldn't start hustling on the streets."

"Relax," I say, laughing. "I'm not gonna."

"Then why? Who are you trying to impress? Do you need to get laid again?"

"No, why do you think that? Can't a girl just change her outfit every once in a while?"

"Depends if that girl is actually a fucking whore." She sighs. "Hailey, you're not a real ho. I know I said that, but it was only a joke."

I place a hand on her shoulder. "Chill. I know you were. I'm not gonna be a real hooker. I don't have anyone to impress." I walk past her.

"Well, you're sure not yourself all right, that I do know." She sighs. "But I can see this makes you happy, I guess? So if you're happy, then I am too."

I don't wanna talk about it right now. Maybe I'll tell her about Thomas and me sometime, but not today. "Great. Now, are you coming?"

She checks the clock, confused. "Um, we still have like thirty minutes. Why the rush?"

"I wasn't there the last two times, so I wanna catch up on homework."

"Okay." She frowns, and I get the feeling she sees straight through my charade.

"See ya in a little bit then?"

"Yeah, whatever. You go on ahead. I'll be there. Don't worry."

I nod and wave as I go out the door and run down the stairs.

I don't know why, but I'm smiling from ear to ear. Maybe it's the nerves of being looked at because literally everyone I pass turns their head.

Or maybe it's because I can't wait to see the look on his face the moment *he* sees me.

Because that's the only thing I can think about right now as I'm walking to his classroom.

How I can make his eyes focus solely on me.

How I can get him hard just by looking at me.

How I affect him.

Because that's what I like the most about our exchanges. The attention he's giving me, something no one else ever has.

I take a deep breath and then open the door to the classroom, only to find it empty. I take another good look, but he really isn't there. I walk along the corridor, passing all the doors which have small metal plates attached to them with names scribbled on them. Finally, the fifth door has *Thomas Hard* engraved on the plate.

I reach for the handle, but then I realize he might be busy, and I don't want to disturb him.

Weird.

I normally want to disturb everyone.

I normally enjoy making people mad.

But not him.

Definitely not him.

Well, maybe … maybe a little bit.

I mean, that spanking sure shook me up.

I'm not sure if I liked it or not. If it was painful or arousing. It was embarrassing. And still, I can't stop wondering if he'll ever do it again … because my heart pumps faster from just the thought.

"Come in." His booming voice makes my face light up.

I push open the door and stand in the middle, waiting for him to look up at me, and when he does … the look on his face makes me want to bend over his desk again.

Fuck me, it's so wrong.

I'm wrong, but fuck it.

"And?" I say.

"Wow …" he mutters, raising his brow at me. "You really went for it, didn't you?"

"Uh-huh …" I take a step inside.

He scoots back his chair and stands up, eyeing me from a distance. "Close the door."

I do what he asks and then walk toward his desk as he steps out from behind it.

"A bit overboard, don't you think?" he muses, adjusting the buttons of his shirt as if they were loose.

I shrug and lean against his desk with my back. "You asked for it."

"I asked for you to dress sexy ..." He stands in front of me.

"And this isn't sexy?" I open my hands and show off my outfit.

The left side of his lip perks up into a seductive smile, and I hold my breath as he leans in. "It's *too* sexy."

Chapter 11

THOMAS

I can't believe she actually did what I said.

Well, it's a little on the extreme side, but I appreciate the effort.

Besides, it's not every day that I see her wearing something like this. I have to relish it.

"So ..." she mumbles.

"You're finally on time ..." I muse.

"Yeah, well ..." She grabs a strand of her hair and toys with it.

I grasp her wrist just before she tucks the strand behind her ear. "Don't. I like it better when it's loose."

She slowly brings her hand down, but I'm still holding her wrist, and I'm not about to let go.

I place my other hand on the table beside her and lean

in.

"You made me spank you yesterday," I murmur. "Why aren't you angry? Afraid?"

"Because you're not dangerous. Not to me," she says, her eyes so seductive they make me want to kiss her.

"I am when you disobey me."

"Do you do this with all your students?" she asks, closing her eyes as I inch closer.

"What? The spanking or the dress code?"

"Both ..."

"I've never done either with anyone but you ..." I whisper.

Her lips are so close, I can almost taste them.

Fuck that, I already can.

I slam my mouth into hers and take her sweet little lips, claiming her as mine.

I don't give a shit that I punish her for being late.

I don't give a shit that I'm supposed to be her teacher.

And I sure as hell don't give a shit that anyone could find us here.

My kiss is soft and sensual, as I don't want to rush it, but it's becoming so hard to resist. I wish I could say that every kiss would be the last. That every time I see her would be the final time. That every day I think of her, it would be as a student and not someone I crave.

But I can't.

I can't fucking stop thinking about her in a way I shouldn't.

Keeping distance is impossible when she needs to be here every goddamn time ... And when she throws her assets in my face like that. But maybe fucking my frustration over not having her out of my system will work.

I grab her waist and set her on the table. She giggles, but I silence her with a kiss. My tongue sweeps out to lick her lips, which part eagerly, allowing me entry. I suck on her lips and let my tongue roam free around her mouth, licking the roof of her mouth.

Panting, I take my lips off hers for a second to admire the glow on her face.

I know she wants this too.

I don't have to ask, and she doesn't need to tell. It's written all over her face.

"You're a naughty girl … you know that?" I murmur, and then I press another kiss to her neck.

"I know what I am; you don't need to tell me."

"And mouthy too." I suck so hard it makes her moan.

The red mark left on her skin makes me smile. "You'll have to tell your friend another boy did that."

"Why?" She frowns.

"Because this can't happen and it's not. Do you understand?"

"You mean we're not kissing right now?" she says with a wicked smile on her face.

"Exactly." I grin and then place another kiss on her lips. "We're not kissing at all."

I leave her lip with a final tiny bite and then slide my fingers up her skirt, far enough to tickle her sweet pussy through the fabric of her panties.

She bites her lip and sucks in a breath.

"Like that?" I ask.

She nods sweetly.

I hook my fingers around her panties and pull them

down slowly, taking delight in the sight of her naked pussy appearing underneath. "Do you know what else we're not doing?" My hand dives between her legs, and I cup her pussy. "I'm not touching your sweet little pussy right now. And we're definitely not going to fuck right now."

She moans into my mouth when I rub her softly.

"God, you're such a tease," I whisper. "Always being late, getting me all riled up."

"I can't help it. Your class is just that boring," she says.

"Now, you're just trying to get me mad." I swat her legs. "Open."

"Ow …" she murmurs.

"I told you not to make me angry."

"Yeah, well, you've been an asshole too, so …"

I cock my head. "When was I an asshole to you?"

"When you said you didn't know there were students coming to the bar and that you needed to find another place to chill."

"Oh … yeah, well, your friend was with you there. I needed to say something."

She purses her lips but then closes her eyes. Whether she accepts my explanation doesn't really matter.

All that matters is that I want her. Now.

"Enough talking." I nudge her legs further apart and slide my index finger up and down her slit until her wetness coats my fingers. Then I flick her clit, watching her eagerly as she moans softly.

I place one hand over her mouth. "Shhh …" I mutter. "Don't want anyone hearing you come, now do you?"

She shakes her head.

I toy with her until she's swollen and panting, then I

insert a finger. She gasps, sucking on the inside of my fingers as I keep my hand firmly over her mouth to prevent the noise from escaping.

"I know you want to moan … And trust me when I say there's nothing in this world I'd want to hear more than your moan. But students are out there, and that door isn't locked."

Her eyes tear away for a second, a sliver of terror flashing through them, so I distract her with the thrusts of my finger. I fuck her with one until she's calmed down, and then I add another so she can feel the fullness. I go on until she's shaking, her toes curling as she reaches the edge.

"Are you a dirty girl, Hailey? Are you going to soak my desk with your wetness?"

She nods, moaning against my hand.

"Shhh … no sound. Just come from my fingers. All over my hand …"

She quivers and her eyes roll back for a second. Then her muscles contract around my fingers, and a flood of wetness gushes out of her. My cock springs erect from the sight.

"Good …" I whisper as she takes sharp breaths through her nose. "Good girl. You did so well."

I remove my hand from her mouth and take my fingers from her pussy. I can't help myself; I bring them to my nose and smell them. Something about the scent of a horny woman just turns me on like nothing else. God, it only makes me want to fuck her more.

I bring my fingers to my lips and dip my tongue out to take just the tiniest of licks.

That's it.

Enough to bring out the beast and let it take control. "My turn."

I grasp her tight white button up and rip it open. One of the buttons at the top flies off, scattering away, but I pay no attention to it. With one sweep, everything—including pens, paperwork, and a stapler—flies off my desk. She squeals as I push her down on my desk and pull down her bra, exposing her pink, hardened nipples.

Licking my lips, I say, "So innocent ... and to think you were still a virgin when we met."

"I've touched boys before," she suddenly blurts out.

"What?" I frown.

"Well, they touched me, and I touched them ... but I never fucked before you. Um ... never mind. TMI."

"Yes, it is," I mutter, and I tug at one of her nipples with my index finger and thumb. "And none of those boys compare, do they?"

"No, oh god, no." Her tone is a mixture of pain and pleasure. Just the way I like it.

"You're fucking with a grown man, Hailey. Think you can handle it?" I tug at her nipples until a small cry escapes her mouth.

"Yes! If you'd stop torturing me so much and just fuck me all right. Dammit."

"There's one thing you should learn about me, Hailey, and that's never to talk back to me like that. Because I *will* make you pay." I twist her nipples and release them, only to do it twice.

"Fuck! All right, all right. Yes, fuck. You're right. I won't. I'm sorry."

"Good. Now ... spread your legs for me. Show me what

a good girl you can be."

Tentatively, she parts her legs, probably unsure of what I'm going to do with her.

But I only have one thing in mind.

I reach into my pocket, fish out my wallet, and take out the spare condom I always carry with me. Just in case. Not to randomly fuck people, of course. I would never. But I always like to come prepared, for instances like this.

I pull down my zipper and pull out my cock. Then I rip open the packet and roll it over my length.

"Oh, god ..." She tilts her head and looks up, her eyes widening at the sight of me.

"It came in you before, you can do it again," I muse, smiling at her. "And if you want to get real frisky, I'll fuck your tiny ass too."

"What?" Her jaw drops.

"Don't worry, I'll save it for later ... along with all the other things I have planned." I can't help lopsided smile on my face when I see the fear in her eyes. I never realized it was this fun to fuck virgins until I fucked her.

"Planned? I thought this would be a one-time only thing."

"Oh, fuck no ..." I say, as I rub my cock along her pussy.

She moans. "But you said ... something about professionalism ..."

"Fuck professionalism," I retort. "I can't do it anymore."

"... and teacher-student relationship," she adds.

I lick my lips. "Exactly. Teacher-student relationship. Because I'm going to teach you how to fuck and be fucked.

Now, stay still."

I line myself up to her and thrust. She gasps and grips her tit with one hand. I smirk and pull out, only to thrust again. Grabbing her legs, I fuck her hard and fast, pounding into her with every inch of me.

Sweat drips down my forehead as I shove my cock into her, wanting to claim every inch of her.

I don't know what it is about this girl that makes me so wild, so crazy and lustful, but I'm not going to fight it any longer. She's a grown woman; she can take it.

"Fuck, you're so tight," I murmur as I slam into her. "Look at me, Hailey. Look at me when I fuck your pussy like it should be fucked."

"Oh, god. If sex is always like this, I need it every day," she says, making me laugh a little.

"It can be if you want it to be," I say.

I put my fingers on her clit and flick, making her moan out loud.

"I want you to come again. Let me feel it with my cock."

"Jesus, you're the only man I've ever met who's wanted me to come this badly," she says.

"You met boys, Hailey. Boys. I'm not a fucking boy, and I sure don't fuck like one." I smack her tit, which makes her squeal.

"Fuck you!" she yells. "Why'd you do that?"

"Because I"—I slap her other tit—"don't tolerate your bad words. It's time you learned how to behave, and if you don't want to listen, then maybe I can fuck it into you."

"That makes no sense," she says.

"Keep talking and I'll spank your ass tomorrow too," I growl, her back talk causing me to fuck her even harder.

"You're not even teaching our class tomorrow."

"Doesn't. Matter. I'm taking what I want, when I want, and you'll give me anything I demand. Are. We. Clear?" Each word is another slap.

"Yes."

I reach for her clit and rub it between two fingers. "Yes, what?"

"Yes, Sir!" she moans.

"Good. Keep it up and maybe I'll be a little nicer." I thrust into her so deeply the desk shakes. "Or is that the opposite of what you want? Because you like it when I'm rough with you, don't you? You like getting your pussy pounded like you're some kind of fuck-doll."

"Fuck, yes," she says, as I grab her waist with both hands and shove my cock into her pussy, which fits me like a glove.

"You're a dirty little thing. My fuck-doll. My pussy to fuck whenever I please. And this pussy is gonna come for me too. Isn't it?"

"Yes … Yes, oh god." Her body quakes underneath me.

"Then do it. Come all over my cock, you filthy girl."

She moans out loud and then I feel her muscles contract all around my length. I thrust into her once more and feel the cum burst out of me. I groan out loud, seed spilling out of me as I pound into her a few more times.

When the orgasm subsides, I take out my cock and pull off the condom. I drag her off the desk and make her bend over it again, pushing her body down as my arousal is still at its limit. Then I pour the contents of the condom over the desk, right in front of her.

"Lick it."

"What?" she mutters.

I grab her hair and nudge her closer to my cum. "Clean my desk."

She looks mad ... madly sexy as her mouth opens and her tongue dips out.

Slowly but surely, she starts licking the cum, swiping her tongue along the wood.

"Don't leave a drop," I growl. "Understood?"

"Yes, Sir ..." she says, eyeing me from the side, but I ignore it.

She'll learn who's in charge. Besides, I can tell from the way she runs her tongue along her mouth after swallowing that she enjoys my taste.

When all the spots are gone, she licks the desk once more and then stands up. "All done."

"Good girl." I hold my dick out in front of her. "Now clean me."

She hesitates for a second, but then her tongue dips out, and I shove my cock into her mouth. She moans a little as I slather my dick all over her tongue, making sure every last bit of cum is inside her mouth. She's enjoying it a little too much, though, almost making me want to have another go.

Better not. I have more things to do today besides fucking her.

"Swallow," I tell her when I pull out.

When she does what I ask, I smile and throw the empty condom in the bin, deciding I'll cover it up later. Then I tuck my spent and satisfied cock back into my pants.

Panting, I slide aside a lock of her hair and tuck it behind her ear, lingering so I can caress her cheek. She looks at me with rosy cheeks and eyes that look a bit glossy.

"How was it?" I ask.

A grin appears on her face. "Good."

I narrow my eyes. "The taste of my cum or the sex?"

"Both."

"You okay?"

"Yeah … just a little … wowed."

I laugh. "Okay, well, as long as you don't share that wow with anyone else, I'm good."

"Share?" She grabs her panties off the floor and puts them back on again. "I don't have any other boys in my life right now, if that's what you mean."

I frown. "Not what I meant, and I'm sure as hell not fucking jealous."

"Okay, well, sorry," she scoffs, raising her brows at me.

I let out a sigh. "Don't take it badly. I didn't mean it that way."

"Right, of course." She shakes it off like she's already over it, but I can tell she's not. "Well, we fucked. End of story. Time for class."

She tries to pass me, but I grab her arm to stop her. "Wait."

"Why?"

"You're misunderstanding me. That shit came out wrong." I pull her toward me and grab her shoulders. "I'm not jealous of any boy … because I know you don't want them. And what I meant with 'not sharing' is that we need to keep this a secret." I tip up her chin and smile. "Can you do that for me?"

"You mean not even telling Lesley?"

"Not telling anyone." I lean in closer. "This could kill my career. Get you expelled."

"Oh ... right ..." Her eyes drift off. "Because you're still my teacher and I'm your student."

I grab her by the waist and pull her closer. "Hey, look at me." I wait until she does. "Just because I am doesn't mean this whole thing doesn't mean anything. It does."

"But it's just sex," she adds.

"Yes ..." I sigh, trying to make peace with the fact that it's *just* sex.

That it *should* be just sex.

But for some reason, something gnaws at my insides when I hold her like this.

"So ... guess we should get to the classroom then?" she asks.

"Not yet ... there's one more thing ..."

"If you wanna know ... no, I didn't do my homework. Wanna spank me now? Jizz in my panties again?"

I smirk. "No, but thanks for telling me. I'll remember it the next time my hand gets itchy."

She gives me an awkward smile, followed by a raised eyebrow, almost as if she's trying to outplay me, but it isn't happening.

My fingers are still locked around her chin, and I pull her closer until my lips touch hers and her breath is stolen by me.

Capturing her mouth with mine makes me numb with desire, even after just fucking her into oblivion. I don't know what it is about her, but she makes me want to latch on and never let go.

That is until someone knocks on my door and opens it in about two seconds time ...

Catching us in the act.

"Mr. Hard, did you—"

Our lips unlock, and a gasp escapes Hailey's mouth as she turns her head toward the sound.

My eyes are drawn toward the girl standing in the door, her pupils dilating the longer she stares.

"Oh, my god." Hailey whispers. "Lesley?"

Chapter 12

Hailey

Fuck.

"O ... kay ..." Lesley mutters as she stands stupefied in the doorway. "I'll just go to class."

"Wait!" I yell, unhooking myself from Thomas's embrace. I run to her and grab her arm. "Please ..."

"Sorry, I didn't mean to intrude," she says, trying to walk away, but I keep going after her.

"Please, let me explain."

"Explain what?" She suddenly comes to a stop and turns around. "You were kissing Mr. Hard. What's there to explain?"

"I know what you saw, but it isn't what you think."

"What I think? I'm not thinking anything. I'm trying *not*

to think because all I can come up with is how ... awkward it is. Sure, I fantasized about hooking up with a teacher, but actually doing it is a whole different story. This is just ... weird."

"I'm sorry you had to see us like that. Please, can we go talk somewhere in private?" I ask, grabbing her hand.

"I don't know ..." She bites her lip. "Fine, but only if you tell me exactly what's going on. No lies."

I nod and take her to a small corner where no one else seems to bother coming. "Look. Thomas and I ... Mr. Hard, we've been involved for a few days now."

"You mean this has been going on longer than just today?" She makes a face. "Is this because I told you to look at his ass?" She narrows her eyes. "I didn't know you'd actually jump on him."

"No ..." I shush her. "Be quiet. I don't want anyone else to hear."

She frowns. "Well, you could've kissed somewhere else too, but you didn't. I was only going to ask him if he'd already graded my papers, and then I found you two smooching like two crazy lovebirds."

"I know how it must look to you, but I'm not using him, and he isn't using me."

She places her hand on her side. "Then why? Why would you hook up with him? You know he's your teacher, right?"

"No shit, I haven't forgotten. Why do you think we were hiding?"

"Good job hiding with the door unlocked, dimwit."

We throw each other shade until we both sigh.

"Okay ... I meant to tell you, but ..." I take a deep

breath. "Thomas is actually the same guy I fucked a few days ago. The one from the club that I told you about."

She takes in a sharp breath. "No ..."

"Yes."

She leans in. "The one who took your virginity?"

"Uh-huh."

"No ..."

I chuckle a little. "Yes. How many times do you want me to say it?"

"I don't fucking believe it," she says.

"Well, you'd better because it's the truth."

"Oh my god ..."

"I know; it's a bit hard to believe I had sex with our professor."

"You've been lying to me all this time ..." she says, pursing her lips.

"No, I just didn't tell you. Big difference."

"How could you not tell me? It's like the single most important detail."

"I didn't know, okay? I didn't know he was my professor. And when I did find out, I felt so humiliated; I just wanted to forget about it."

"Oh, my god ..." She puts her hand over her forehead like she just got a premonition. "So that's why you left when we had our first class. You said you were sick." She points at me. "Lie."

"Guilty." I raise my hands. "Look, I'm sorry. I really didn't mean to lie to you. It just ... happened."

"Like you just *happened* to fuck your goddamn teacher."

I shrug, and she rolls up a paper in her hand and slaps me on the head, making me laugh. "Are you outta your mind?" she yells. "Do you even know how stupid this all sounds?"

"Yes! Stop," I say, still laughing, trying to snatch the paper, but she's way quicker than I am.

"You fucked your fucking teacher. If that isn't fifty shades of fucked up, I don't know what is."

"Well … he does like kinky shit." I burst out into more laughter when I see her face all scrunched up.

"Oh my god, that is not the fucking point!" She smacks me again. "You lied!"

"Okay, I get it, and I'm sorry," I say, finally managing to steal the paper from her.

"I just caught you kissing our goddamn teacher."

"I know, and I'm fucking embarrassed."

She frowns. "Then why are you even coming close to him? Why even put yourself in that position? It only makes it harder."

"Well, I can't *not* come to class, can I?"

"Not. What. I. Mean." She takes the paper back and tucks it into her backpack.

"Yes, we kissed. And it's probably not the last time either."

She cocks her head. "That's what I mean. It's not an accident if it happens twice."

"Okay. You're right. I can't resist him."

"And he can't resist you either …" she muses. "So what are you gonna do now? You can't continue this. You know it's not allowed."

"I know, but … I don't know if I can stop. If I really want to."

She's quiet for a second, but the look on her face says it

all.

"Can you forgive me for lying to you?"

Her lips turn to thin lines. "I don't know ..."

"Do I have to beg you?" I pout, which makes her forcefully push away her smile.

"Fine, I forgive you for lying, but that doesn't mean what you're doing is okay."

"I know, but please don't judge me."

"I'm not judging. I'm disappointed. I'm worried about you," she says, swallowing. "I thought you lost your virginity to some random guy, not our damn teacher. This is so awkward. Like how are you gonna sit in class knowing he's seen you naked?"

I raise my brows and slam my lips together, shrugging.

"You haven't even thought about it? What about the consequences? What if someone finds out?"

"You found out ..." I mutter.

"Exactly. So basically, you're already screwed."

"Please, don't tell anyone," I plead, putting up my pouty face. "Please?"

She sighs. "You're asking me to be your accomplice?"

"I'm only asking if you can just pretend you never saw anything."

"But I did." She raises one brow.

"Please ..." I grab her hand. "Promise me you won't tell anyone."

"It's against school policy. It could get you kicked out. It could get him fired. Why do you wanna risk it?" she asks, cocking her head sympathetically.

"Because I ..." I look down at the floor. "He gives me something no one else ever has. I need it." I look up at her.

"Please understand. This is the only way I can deal with my life right now."

"With him?"

"I need this. I need … whatever it is that he's offering."

She lets out a short sigh and nods slowly. "All right. I get it."

"So you'll keep it a secret?"

"Fine, yes, but I don't wanna be involved in anything." She grabs my arm. "I'm not gonna vouch for you if shit goes down. I can't lie for you. I can keep it a secret, but I'm not gonna put my reputation or my spot in college on the line."

"I understand, and I won't ever ask that of you. I just want this to stay under the radar. That's all."

"All right." She nods. "God. I'll need some bleach to rinse that image from my eyes."

I smile. "At least you didn't see us fuck."

"Oh, god, don't start." She turns around but pauses, only to grab my arm again. "But he did have a nice ass, right?"

I grin. "Like Christian Bale nice."

She laughs but then shakes her head. "I thought I wanted to know what was under there, but now, I don't."

"That's just because I tapped that." I wiggle my brows, making her roll her eyes.

"Oh, shut up." She playfully shoves me, and I shove her back.

"So … just for the record … we all right?"

She turns her head toward me. "Were we ever?"

"No …" I say, and since we both know exactly what we mean, we burst out into laughter as we walk through the hallway on our way to the most awkward class we'll ever have.

***

An hour later

Thomas has been staring at me since class started. I know that type of stare, and it isn't good.

It's not the usual I-want-to-fuck-you-to-death stare, but one I've never seen before, and it resembles more of a I'm-going-to-lose-my-shit-in-front-of-everyone stare.

One that makes me wanna crawl under my desk and hope I'll find the door to Narnia.

I can already feel the icy chill from miles away, and it makes me shiver in place.

"Cold?" Lesley asks. "I have a scarf if you want."

"No, just feeling watched." I nod at her and then at Thomas.

Her mouth forms an o-shape. "Oh ... must be because I ..."

"Yep." I nod. "I can't wait for this class to end."

She chuckles. "What did you do? Bite his lip?"

"Class is over," Thomas suddenly says, and before I can answer Lesley, she's already gotten up from her seat.

"Where are you going?" I ask.

"Library. I'm study buddies with Layla." She packs her bag quickly and shuffles away. "Sorry, I think I forgot to tell you."

"No, it's fine. Go study. I'll just pretend I'm not here. Hopefully, I can sneak out unnoticed."

She makes a face. "I doubt it." Then nods toward

Thomas.

The moment I lay my eyes on him, I just want to die.

That look on his face.

Wow.

"Well, see ya!" Lesley yells, and she's out.

Along with all my other classmates.

And now, I'm left alone with him.

Just like that.

I frantically start packing my shit, trying to be as quick as possible, but apparently, it's still not quick enough.

"Hailey."

His low, blazing voice makes me look, even when I don't really want to.

Oh, god. He's coming over here.

Sweat drips off my forehead as I throw everything in my bag and stand up ... only to come face to face with him.

"Sit. Down."

I swallow and immediately sink back into my chair.

I don't even know why I listen to him. Why he makes me *want* to listen.

Is it fear?

No.

It's not seduction either because he seems pissed.

No ... I think it's ... respect.

Just that admission alone makes me do a double take.

"That girl you were sitting next to. Lesley. You know her well?"

"She's my best friend," I say.

He bends over and places his hand on my desk, cornering me. "She saw us kiss. You went after her. What did you tell her?"

"I asked her if she could keep it quiet," I say.

"What else?" he asks.

"Nothing …"

"There must be something else," he snaps. "How do we know if we can trust her?"

"We can. She'd never betray my trust."

"How do you know for sure?"

I frown from his attitude. "She's my *best* friend. I don't know about you, but to me, that means something."

His lips twitch. "Don't tell me what it means. I know damn well. I just want to make sure she's not going to tell the whole world about us."

"Why? Are you afraid someone could find out?"

"Of course, I am!" he yells. "It could ruin my career."

"Obviously. That's all that's important."

He sighs. "That's not what I said. I just don't want to risk it." He cocks his head. "You should understand. This could ruin you too."

I make a face. "I told you that you could trust her. You should trust me too."

His lips part but then he slams them shut again, growling to himself. "Fuck. We should've locked that goddamn door when we could."

"Look, I'm sorry, okay? I didn't know she'd come and see you. She never used to be that interested in knowing her grades."

"Grades? This was about grades? That's why she saw us kissing?" He throws his hand in front of his eyes and slowly slides it down his face. "God-fucking-dammit." He slams the table so hard it makes me jolt up in my seat.

"Jesus," I shout.

"Fuck." He turns away, his shoulders rising each time he takes a breath.

The tension in the room is killing me.

"You don't have to be so mad."

"Well, I am." He turns to me again. "Look, I care a lot about my reputation."

"I can see that," I sneer. "Is that why you had sex with me? To boost your reputation?"

He puts his hand down right in front of me again. "You know damn well that you didn't know I was your teacher, and I didn't know you were my student. I would've never fucked you if I did."

"Oh, really now? So you regret fucking me? Thanks for telling me."

He sighs and growls again, turning around to collect his rage. "I don't regret fucking you. And fucking you isn't a fucking loss of my reputation. It's the fact that people find out."

"So you want to fuck me … only in secret," I say.

"Didn't we already establish that?" he asks, narrowing his eyes. "No, Hailey, I don't regret anything. Except Lesley finding out about us. And that makes me very angry."

"I can see …" I raise a brow and turn my head.

He takes another deep breath. "Okay … just … make sure she doesn't talk. To anyone. About us."

"She won't," I say.

"Just keep an eye on her," he says, looking straight at me. "If this gets out …"

"It won't."

He closes his eyes, remaining quiet for a couple of seconds. "Okay, look. I think we need to quit."

"Quit? What?" My jaw drops. "Why? Are you angry at me or something?"

"No, I'm not mad at you," he says, balling his fist. "I'm angry with myself. For letting it get this far. For letting her see us."

"I told you it won't happen again."

"You don't know that. It could be someone else. Anyone. This whole thing could blow up," he says.

"So you just wanna give up? Quit?"

"Yes." He takes another sharp breath. "It was fun, Hailey. While it lasted."

"Fun …" I repeat.

The way he puts it makes my stomach feel like someone's grasping and constricting it.

"Yes. And I mean that in a good way." He leans in and grabs a loose strand of my hair, tucking it behind my ear. "I like you, Hailey. And I did enjoy it while it lasted."

"While it lasted? I don't like this."

"Well, I'm sorry, but this is my call."

"And I don't have any say in it?" I say, making a face.

"Unfortunately not."

"Fuck no," I say.

"Please …" He rubs his eyes with his index finger and thumb. "Please, don't make this any more difficult."

"Difficult? Like it's so fucking difficult to call it quits."

"To me it is," he snaps.

"Well, I don't agree, Thomas." I fold my arms, giving him my cheeky, non-agreeable gaze, which he hates so much.

"That's the last time you'll call me that," he says. "It's Mr. Hard. Remember it."

He turns around, and as he walks away, I yell out, "Why? So no one will know we were on a first-name basis?"

"We never were," he says, glancing at me over his shoulder. "I am, and will always be, Sir to you."

"Yeah, well you know what else? I think I'm gonna call you Mr. Fuck. Because that's what you are. A fucking asshole."

He narrows his eyes at me but doesn't respond as he keeps walking.

"I think I'll call you Sir Asshole! Sir Dickwad! Sir Go-Fuck-Yourself!"

But no matter what I call him, he won't come to spank me for it.

He won't even turn around to look at me.

Fuck.

Chapter 13

THOMAS

I didn't want to be an asshole to her, but what else was I supposed to do when faced with such a threat?

That girl knows about us.

Not just the kissing part, but the fucking part too, no doubt. Hailey would tell her best friend everything. God, it was only a matter of time before it came out.

I sink into my couch and grab my rum off the table, taking a much-needed sip.

I wish it could've been more simple.

That I could just fuck girls without there being a consequence, but there always is.

Lies. Anger. Bittersweet good-byes.

It's always there, even when I fight so damn hard not to

have any of it.

I don't want to feel these things.

And I fucking *hate* feeling caught.

Maybe I should just give up fucking once and for all.

I take another sip and stare out the window.

Like I ever could.

I love sex too much to give it up.

But I should definitely be more careful who I approach from now on.

Had I known the club was a place students would come, I would've never have gone there. I wouldn't have risked it. Not that it was completely my fault because she was there when she wasn't supposed to be. She isn't even twenty-one yet. She's not supposed to drink.

Not that I should be surprised.

Hailey doesn't listen to rules.

Maybe that's why she fascinates me so much.

It's probably also why I can't stop thinking about her.

I like her tenacity. Her unyielding nature. Like she could fight off the world and still not give up.

Maybe it's something I've always missed in my life.

Because I did give up.

Once.

I take another sip but follow it with a full chug.

I need another drink.

Instead, I grab my laptop and start stalking her profile again.

I know it's fucking wrong … but I need something to numb myself, and alcohol is not the right choice.

Only when I look through her pictures do I notice the green circle next to her name. She's online.

Without thinking, I open our messages and send her something.

Thomas: Be on time next class. I have important homework.

Hailey: Why are you still messaging me?

Thomas: Because I can.

Hailey: Isn't it unprofessional to message students on Facebook?

Thomas: I'm not going to let you change the topic. You *will* be on time for my next class.

Hailey: Or else?

I ball my fists and sigh, biting my lip in the process. Goddamn this girl. She keeps getting under my skin, and she knows it. That's why she's acting this way. To make me mad. Well, it's working all right.

Hailey: Oh, right … nothing because there is no 'or else' anymore. Pity.

Thomas: Stop.

Hailey: No, you started it. You messaged me. Have nothing better to do? Oh wait, it must be because you're bored.

Thomas: Keep pushing and you'll have extra homework to dig through.

Hailey: Don't care. I won't do it anyway.

Thomas: You. Will. Trust me on that.

My fingers hurt from typing so fast. God, what I wouldn't give to be able to bend her over my leg and spank her hard right now.

Hailey: Really? And who's going to make sure? You? How? With words?

I can already hear her laughter.

Thomas: Just because I ended things, doesn't mean I don't care.

Hailey: You don't get to have your cake and eat it too.

Thomas: Watch me.

My anger gets the best of me as I slam the laptop shut and throw it beside me on the couch.
Growling out loud, I get to my kitchen and reach for the bottle of rum, taking a sip without pouring it into a glass first.
Fuck glasses.
I need some heavy liquor to get me through this.

My cat suddenly jumps up onto the table, scaring the living shit out of me.

"Ninja! Fuck. Why do you always have to do that?" I yell at him, but when he purrs and rubs his face against my hand, I instantly forgive him.

Something about cat love makes it impossible to ignore.

I pick him up and cuddle with him, like real grown-up men do, because fuck masculinity.

Giving my cat love doesn't make me any less of a man.

I have my huge dick to prove that for me.

I smirk as I set Ninja back down and rummage in the drawer to take out his favorite play toy. A miniature dildo that rolls around on the floor.

"Go play with the dildo!" I jest, laughing as I throw it away, and he immediately jumps after it.

Suddenly, my phone buzzes.

I pick it up from the table next to my door and check the messages.

It's a picture sent through Facebook from none other than Hailey Walters.

And it's her fucking ass.

Naked.

On a fucking table.

With a middle finger sticking up from her back.

I put the bottle down to stop myself from throwing it across the room.

Thomas: Have you lost your mind?

Hailey: I just wanted to give you a taste of what you're gonna miss.

Thomas: I'm not missing anything. You're acting like a child.

Hailey: Maybe you shouldn't have treated me like a kid then.

Thomas: Do you even know how dangerous this is?

Hailey: What? Sending you pictures? It can't be any more dangerous than fucking at school.

She has a point there.
But ... she's not doing this to make a point.
She just wants to piss me off.

Thomas: Don't send me more.

Hailey: Why? Making you uncomfortable? Poor you.

I close my phone and clench my teeth. I sit back down on the couch and turn on the television, determined not to get distracted. However, each time the phone buzzes, I can't help but wonder what she sent now.
Curiosity eventually kills the cat.
Well, not my own cat, of course.
It's just a fucking figure of speech.
I open my laptop and check Facebook.
I regret it instantly.
I don't think I've ever seen this many swear words in one conversation. Some are even British and make me

chuckle. I have to admit, the girl's brave. I close my laptop again, determined not to pay any more attention to it.

Except she doesn't stop.

Not in the middle of the night.

Not the next day.

Or the day after.

Or the entire week, for that matter.

It's driving me nuts.

Pictures of her flood my inbox, ranging from middle fingers to actual pussy and titty pictures. Her ass is everywhere, in strange positions, and with a variety of tools and toys, almost as if to mock me. I try to ignore it, even though it makes my blood boil.

She makes it impossible when she shows up in class in a tight red dress. Every boy in class looks at her like she's some sort of sex bomb, their hungry little eyes and drooling mouths making me break a fucking Sharpie.

I get it. She's fucking sexy, and now that she's discovered it herself, she won't give me or anyone else a break. The way she prances around class, showing off her best assets, has gotten my attention, all right.

To the point of me giving the entire class extra homework.

Now, everybody's pissed off.

Well, at least I'm not the only one.

When class ends, I want to call her back and tell her to stay for extra study time. Real study time. If I can't punish her my way, I'll punish her the old-fashioned way.

"Hailey," I yell as she's the last one to leave with Lesley.

She sticks up her middle finger, not even granting me one look.

Shaking my head, I laugh.

I guess telling a girl you want to quit the random sex really does piss her off.

She just doesn't realize she's not the only one who misses it.

But just because I miss it doesn't make it the right choice.

Not with so much on the line.

Every time I look at that girl, Lesley, I wonder if she's going to burst one day … And then everyone will know what I've done. My life will be over.

Again.

I just fucking can't.

So I go back home, still moody as fuck, and surrender myself to a bottle of whiskey instead. Ninja is there to greet me with his usual squeaky meow, which sounds more like he's whining for pussy than anything else.

"I know what you're going through, boy," I tell him, patting him on the head.

He rubs against my leg and then drops in front of my feet, rolling around on the floor to show me his balls. They're huge, as always. I guess we have more than just the lack of pussy in common.

I settle for sitting on the couch after which Ninja joins me, pressing his gigantic balls on my lap. I don't really give a shit, so I just keep scratching behind his ear while he drools on my shirt. It's what we usually do when we're alone. That, and eat dinner together.

He likes things quiet, just like I do. He also likes to watch television, specifically when there are other kitties on—probably because of the pussy. We would've had a perfect bromance, if it weren't for the fact that he's a cat.

I don't even know why I'm enjoying myself the way I am right now, but I guess the whiskey is doing its thing. Quite effective, if you ask me. I already feel much, much better.

The only thing I need is a quick jerk off, and then it'll all be good again.

My phone buzzes again, and I check the messages to see if it's something important. Instead, it's another pussy picture. Fuck me.

Thomas: Enough. Do you want to get caught or something?

Hailey: Anything to get the point across.

Thomas: And what point is that? Seeing if I'm still attracted to you? You're right, I am, but that doesn't make this okay.

Hailey: Just because it isn't okay doesn't mean it can't be done. I don't care about being caught.

I close the app and put my phone away before I do something I might regret.

I pick up the bottle of whiskey and take another sip straight from the bottle. I don't give a shit if it gets me drunk. I need a good hangover right now to get over her and her sweet pussy. Fuck me, I can't stop thinking about driving my fingers up in her, making her suck my dick for all the nasty shit she said.

My cock is already hard from the thought alone.

Goddammit.

Time for porn.

I grab my laptop and open the browser, but then someone rings my doorbell.

I roll my eyes and sigh out loud as I get up off the couch and walk to the door.

"What do you want?" I say as I open it, but when I see the face in front of me, I freeze. "Natalie …"

"Just checking up on you." She glances sideways over my shoulder. "What are you doing?"

I try to block her view with my body. "Nothing important."

"Hmm … well, aren't you going to invite me in?"

"Depends," I muse.

"On what? If I leave quickly?" She places her hand on the door. "I know what you're doing, Thom. You're hiding again."

I frown. "Why the hell would you think that?"

"I can see the bottle from here, you know …" She raises her brow at me.

"So? Who cares. Yeah, I'm drinking. And I was enjoying myself too until you showed up." I attempt to close the door, but she puts her foot inside.

"Why? Why do you keep doing this? I'm trying to help you." She makes a face. "You know I'm the only one you have left."

"Thanks, but I'm good," I say dryly.

I know what she means. I don't have any friends besides her, and my family is pretty much non-existent.

My mom and dad died in a car accident, and my brother

… well, I prefer not to ever mention him to anyone.

Natalie sighs. "Stop drinking. For god's sake, just try to adjust. Stop wasting your life."

"Oh god, not again." I rub my face with my hand. "Please, just go."

"No, you need to man the fuck up and be the guy you promised you'd be."

"That's it. Go," I growl. When she doesn't move, I yell, "Leave!"

"Can't you see this isn't good for you? I'm the only one looking out for you."

"I don't need your help!" I yell. "All I need is to be left alone!"

I slam the door before she can say anything else.

She's already said more than enough.

I know exactly what I'm doing, and I don't give a shit if it's bad for me.

She has no right coming to my apartment like this.

"Thom—" she murmurs through the door.

"Get the fuck outta here!" I yell back.

I wait until I hear her footsteps disappear, and then I saunter back to the couch, sinking into the pillows with a long, drawn-out sigh.

"Fuck me …" I grab the bottle of whiskey and chug it down.

My brain is still overloaded from all the pent-up rage. Even this bottle of whiskey isn't enough to cull my need for a release. The only other option I can think of is having wild, unbridled sex.

That or a good jerk off.

So I rip down my zipper and take out my cock to play

with it.

Anything to let off the steam.

Plus, my cock quickly stiffens from all those dirty pictures Hailey sent me.

Right when I'm rubbing myself and getting hot and bothered, another buzzing interrupts my business.

It's Hailey … and this time, she sent a picture of her pussy being pleasured by her pink rabbit.

God-fucking-dammit.

Fuck that.

I pull out the camera app and make a picture of my hard cock, held at the base, pre-cum dripping down the tip. Then I send it to her.

It's already too late to change my mind.

My cock is on her fucking phone now.

Hailey: Wow … I wasn't expecting you to actually send anything back.

Thomas: That's what you get for being such a fucking tease.

Hailey: Looks appetizing.

Thomas: Come over then and have a taste.

It takes her a while to respond.

Maybe it's because she didn't expect me to invite her over, either.

Quite frankly, *I* don't even know why I invited her.

But I did.

I don't fucking care about the consequences anymore. Natalie, the school, and everyone else can suck my dick. Including Hailey.

If it gets me fired, so be it. At least, I'll finally be able to touch that sweet ass pussy again ... because, fuck me, now that I've had a taste of what she can offer, I think I'm addicted.

Hailey: You don't mean that.

Thomas: Yes, I do. Come over here. Now.

Hailey: You said we were over.

Thomas: And now, I'm saying you need to be here, in my bed, naked.

Hailey: What if I don't want to?

Thomas: You know you do. Why else did you keep sending me pics?

Hailey: And what if I do? Doesn't mean I'll be at your place anytime soon.

Thomas: You will ... after vexing me for so long. You have no other choice.

Hailey: Really? Since when are you the boss of me?

Thomas: Since you kept provoking me. You pushed me

too far now. I'm done playing this game. You come over here right now, so I can thoroughly spank your ass and then fuck that filthy mouth of yours.

Hailey: Interesting ... But what happens if I don't show up?

Thomas: You know exactly what will happen if you don't show up.

She doesn't respond, but I know I have her.
She can't say no. Neither can I.
And within thirty minutes, she's proven me right.
A knock on the door is all I need. I'd already unlocked and opened the door slightly the moment I got off the phone.
"Come in," I say with that low voice I know she likes.
I turn my head when I hear the door creak and spot her standing in my doorway in a tight, black leather dress and matching heels.
With a smirk on my face, I watch her lips part, and I growl, "Lock the door. I'm going to do bad things to you ..."

Chapter 14

Hailey

I knew it was a bad idea the moment I stepped into his home, but I can't say no to it either.

I need this. I want this. Badly.

Even if it's bad for me.

Even if it's wrong.

When is anything good ever right?

Especially when it's standing in front of a window, half-naked.

When he turns his body toward me, and my gaze lands on his huge, erect cock, I'm sold.

Good god.

He's like a fucking stallion.

It's the first time I've seen him naked … and boy, do I

like it.

It's one of the few times I've ever seen any man naked, for that matter, but he trumps them all.

He doesn't seem the least bit surprised by my dropped jaw, or the flush that stains my cheeks as I try to hide the fact that I'm so totally turned on right now.

"You've been very, very naughty, Hailey." His voice is so gravelly, it makes my legs quiver. Fuck. Me.

"I told you not to make me angry," he continues. "And still you kept sending those pictures."

"But it worked," I say.

"You have no idea what you're doing to me, do you?" He cracks his knuckles.

I swallow away the lump in my throat. "I think I can see …" I point at his cock, which bobs up and down from my attention, making my mouth water.

"Yes, you can …" He slowly starts unbuttoning his shirt, exposing his muscled pecs. "I never undress for a girl, but for you, I will." It sounds like a good thing until he opens his mouth again. "Because you've royally pissed me off."

"Sorry," I say.

"Don't. I know why you did it. You wanted me to regret my decision."

"Do you?" I ask.

He narrows his eyes as he reaches the bottom of his shirt, his fingers briefly just below his navel. "Isn't it obvious?"

"You were being an ass. Of course, I had to return the favor." I take a deep breath. "Any girl with guts would've done the same."

At first, his gaze only intensifies, but then the right side of his mouth tips up into a smile. "And that's exactly why it's impossible for me to stay away."

I take a step toward him, but his rumbling voice makes me stop in my tracks. "Wait. You teased me, Hailey. Toyed with me past my limits. Now, it's my turn." His tongue darts out to wet his lips. "Strip for me."

For a second, I hesitate, but then I drop my bag to the floor and roll up my dress. He wants me to prove how much I still want this? I'll show him. He thinks I've given up because he's been an asshole to me, but I haven't. He's the only solid thing in my life right now, besides Lesley, and I'm not giving it up that easily.

And from the look on his face, I can tell he's not ready to give it up either, despite his earlier claims. He's hungry … biting his lip at the sight of my bra and panties. His cock bounces up and down the moment my bra drops to the floor, and again when I lower my panties and kick them away.

His eyes wander across my body, lavishly taking in my naked skin as if he's savoring the moment. I feel exposed, almost ashamed of being naked. But the smile on his lips makes all my insecurities disappear.

"On your knees," he says with a gritty undertone.

I do what he asks, slowly but surely, still not completely convinced of his dominance over me, even though I know full well what kind of effect he has on me.

He pulls away his shirt and slides it off his shoulders, dropping it on the floor. The chiseled body that appears is nothing short of magnificent. I can't even look away as he grabs something off the table beside the couch and walks toward me. Only when he's right in front of me do I notice the item in his hand. My eyes widen as he shows it to me, smirking.

"I'm going to punish you with this, Hailey. Do you think you can handle it?"

It's a leather paddle.

Oh, my fucking god.

I don't even know how to respond to this.

Thomas bends over and places his hand underneath my chin, tipping it up. "Don't be frightened," he says. "I won't push you beyond your limits," he adds. His hand gently caresses my cheek. "But you need a good spanking, and this is the only way."

"You mean, for you," I say.

He smiles gently. "Exactly. For me. And you will do this because I need you to." He leans in, pressing his lips softly against mine, only to whisper in my mouth. "And if you behave … I'll reward you with a lick."

I shiver from the memory of having his tongue against my clit.

"Now, lift your ass," he says, walking to my other side. "Crawl forward."

I do what he says, placing one hand in front of the other, my knees sliding across his floor.

WHACK!

The paddle that comes down on my ass makes me drop.

"Get up," he says with a soft but stern voice. "Or I'll make it last longer."

I push myself up from the floor and reposition myself.

Again, the paddle comes down, this time on my other ass cheek. It burns and sizzles through my entire body. I can even feel it between my legs.

"Crawl toward the table," he says.

I obey. I don't know why. Maybe it's because I feel humiliated and desperately need to block out my insecurities. Or maybe it's because I honestly do like listening to him. Obeying him. Like a good girl would do when she's smitten with her teacher.

When he hits me again, I groan.

"Having second thoughts?" he muses.

"No ..." I say under a heavy breath.

"Good. Because I'm doing this for the both of us. For your pleasure as well as mine."

WHACK!

Another hit has me moaning out loud.

"See? Pleasure," he says. "You need to learn how to accept things the way they are, especially when it comes to me. And right now, I want to punish your ass for swearing at me. For sending me pictures without permission ... and for behaving like a brat."

He punctuates each sentence with another spanking with the paddle.

My ass feels like it's on fire, but it's a good kind of fire ... the fire that makes me want to touch myself. And it's so goddamn wrong, but I don't care anymore.

"Fuck me ... does your ass look fine with red marks all over it," he growls. "Wait there." He walks to the table beside me and grabs something from it. His hand suddenly comes down on my ass, making me squeal a little.

"Ass up," he says.

I can't help but glance at him, but I immediately regret it too.

There's lube in his hand. And three small, round balls attached to one another.

"What are you going to do?"

He swats me again. "Ah-ah. No questions unless I ask. You'll answer only to me now."

I sigh but don't respond. I know how he likes to play this game. Rough, demanding, and over-the-top domination. I've never been with a guy like that. In fact, none of them were even remotely interested in this type of play. But I have to admit it turns me on like no other. There's just something about listening to a man … not a boy, but a man. Something so primal, so fulfilling that I can't get enough of it.

"These, are Ben Wa balls … the ultimate pleasure for your pussy," he says as he positions himself behind me. "And I'm going to use them to make you come."

Fuck me. Just those words already undo me.

His fingers are suddenly on my slit, spreading the wetness that's already there across my lips. "Hmm … Your pussy seems to enjoy spankings," he teases. "Good thing I like handing them out too."

"I can't help the way my body reacts," I answer.

He smacks my ass close to my entrance, making me quiver with delight.

"No talking unless I tell you to. Do you understand?"

"Yes."

Another smack makes me moan.

"Yes, Sir."

"Good girl," he murmurs.

He slides his fingers up and down my slit until the wetness is everywhere, and then they're gone. I hear the bottle opening, squirts splashing onto his hands, probably to rub on the metal balls.

Except then his index finger is suddenly on my ass.

Lubricated. Slippery.

Pushing into my hole.

"I don't just want to spank you, Hailey ... That would be too easy."

"Oh, my g—" I can't even finish my sentence because of his finger pushing into my puckered hole.

"I told you I'd use your ass sooner or later. But first, I have to prepare you."

"Oh, god ..." I mutter, unable to utter any sensible words after feeling him enter me from behind. It feels so weird, so full, and there's so much resistance. I don't think I can do this.

"Relax, Hailey," he murmurs, placing his hand on my ass to spread my cheeks. "Breathe. This finger isn't the only thing that's going to be in your ass, so you'd better get used to it. The more you fight it, the more it'll hurt."

I nod, trying to compose myself as he pushes farther, but the feeling is so different from when he enters my pussy. So fucking wrong ... but good. Dirty good.

"How does it feel?" he asks when his finger is completely inside me.

"Good, I think?"

"Be certain. What do you feel? There's no need to be ashamed."

"It feels filthy ... but it turns me on too," I say.

He chuckles. "I can tell." Another one of his fingers brushes along my pussy, swiping off the wetness. I can hear him suck it off. "I can *definitely* tell."

I don't know why, but this man can make me fucking

blush.

He pushes into my little hole a few more times, waiting until I relax my muscles before he increases his pace. The more he goes on, the more excited I get. I didn't know having something up your ass could be this satisfying. He really knows how to hit the spot.

"I'm proud of you, Hailey. It's not often a girl accepts me so easily, especially in her ass," he muses. "Now, spread your legs."

He pulls his finger out, leaving me with an empty feeling, which he quickly replaces by thrusting a different finger into my pussy. I moan out loud as he probes me, twisting around inside.

"Yes, make those noises … show me how much you want me to fuck your little holes."

His dirty words make my clit thump with pleasure as he plays with me, cupping my pussy as if he wants to own it completely. And maybe him owning me isn't the worst that could happen to me right now. I'd let him if he asked.

"It's going to feel a bit cold now …" he murmurs, squirting more lube on his hands.

The next thing I feel are the metal balls pushing against my entrance.

I suck on my lip as I feel the first one enter me, and I bite a little when the second one nudges in too. It feels so full inside my pussy and cold, like he said. Like something is melting inside me. It makes me giggle.

"Funny?" he asks.

"A little."

A sudden swat on my ass makes me jolt up and down, and the balls sway against my walls, the intensity through the roof. Just that one slap made me moan with pleasure. Oh, god. I almost came.

"Hmm ... I bet that's sensitive, isn't it?" he says.

"Yeah."

He slaps me again, making me groan and quiver from delight.

"Yes, Sir," I say.

"Good. Remember how to address me. Make me happy ... and I'll make you happy. Do you know what I want?"

"Me?"

"Yes ... but how?"

"On the floor?"

He smacks my ass again, and my head spins with dizziness from the pre-orgasmic pulses. God. He doesn't even have to touch my pussy to make me come this way.

"How?" he repeats.

"I don't know. On the bed?"

Another smack.

"Fuck!"

"Don't you fucking come, Hailey," he growls. "I haven't given you permission."

I don't know the answer. What he wants me to say. All I know is that I'm in a position where I literally wanna beg him to make me come. And no one in my life has ever gotten me to beg.

"Please ..."

Another smack almost pushes me over the edge of bliss.

"Don't. Come." His voice is the only thing I can hold onto that keeps me from tumbling.

It's like a basic instinct. Conforming to him. Obeying his every whim, even if I'll hate him for it.

It's in his voice.

In his touch.

Makes me want to give him everything.

Everything.

That's it!

"How do I want you, Hailey?" he repeats.

"Any way you desire," I reply with a high-pitched voice.

His hand freezes mid-air, then lowers. A tempting smile crossing his lips.

"Hmm ... Finally, you're beginning to learn."

Chapter 15

Hailey

He grabs my hair and pulls until my head tilts back, his finger sliding across my slit. "Does this pussy belong to me?"

"Yes, Sir," I whimper when he reaches my clit.

His finger disappears again, leaving me high and dry.

"Crawl to my bed," he says.

I nod and push my knees in the right direction. Each movement is another filthy reminder of the balls inside me. I think that's why he's telling me to do this. He wants me to feel the intense pleasure until it makes me burst. And then he'll probably still not let me come.

"Stand up at the edge of the bed," he says, walking

behind me.

I do what he says and stand up straight. The balls really push down now, putting ample pressure on my pussy.

"Feels good, doesn't it?" he teases.

"Yes, Sir."

"I can be good to you, Hailey ... but only if you're good to me too. And since you've been so bad, I'm not going to let you come ... yet." I can hear the amusement in his voice, and god, it makes me want to yell at him, but then I'd have to wait even longer for my release, which is the last thing I want.

"No back talk? I'm impressed," he says as he opens his drawer, taking something out. I don't respond. He didn't ask me anything, so I'm going by his rules.

"I'm glad you finally learned that one way or another, you're going to have to listen to me. It's the only way to get what you want ... Me."

He grabs my arms tight. "Put them behind your back."

"What's gonna happen?" I mutter.

He spanks my ass so hard it makes me yelp. "What did I tell you?"

"Sorry ... Sir," I say through gritted teeth.

"But I'll answer your question this time. I'm going to tie you up, and you're going to let me do everything I want to you. Understand?"

I take in a sharp breath when he places my wrists next to each other and wraps something that feels like tough rope around them. "Yes, Sir."

He pulls the rope until it fastens around my wrists, strong enough that I'll be unable to break free without his help. My heart beats in my throat when his hand caresses my ass.

"Afraid?" he asks.

"A little."

"Of what? Nothing will happen that you don't want to happen. But I am going to push your limits."

"The rope …" I mutter.

"Oh … this little thing?" He pulls on it, which makes my body lean back into his arms. His lips are close to my ear when he whispers, "This just makes it easier to control you."

Control.

That's what it's all about.

He craves the power.

It scares me … but it also makes me want to let him play.

Maybe I really am into the kinky shit, even though I didn't know.

"Trust me when I say you'll like every single thing I do …" he whispers into my ear, his tongue darting out to lick my neck. Then he presses a kiss onto my skin, pulling at my hair to make my head dip back, claiming my body as his.

With one push, he manages to shove me down onto the bed, lifting my ass with his arm. A hard spanking follows, but it doesn't hurt anymore. All I can feel are the pleasure beads bouncing inside me.

"Stay," he growls, walking to his cabinet. I glance sideways and watch him rip open a condom, rolling it over his dick.

I nod, saliva running into my mouth at the sight of him walking toward me, his cock erect.

He positions himself behind me and pushes my back down. "Lower. Face against the mattress."

I don't resist. It feels so goddamn raunchy, like I'm being used, but it's so arousing I can't say no.

His fingers slide between my slit, rubbing me so fast, I swear I'm gonna come.

"You want to come?" he asks.

"Yes!" I moan.

"Beg me ..." he says gruffly. "Beg me, and maybe I'll allow it."

"Please ..." I mutter, feeling heady from the heat.

He spanks my ass again, making me groan. "Please, what?"

"Please, make me come."

Another hard whack has me on the edge again. "Say that again."

"Please, can I come, Sir?"

Another smack. My ass burns from his palm. "Louder!"

"Please! Let me come, Sir!" I beg. I am literally begging to be allowed.

Never have I ever let anyone decide anything for me.

Until now.

"Come."

His commanding voice is all I need.

The moment I come, he reaches for the wire between my legs and pulls out the balls.

One. By. One.

Each plop adding more pleasure, flooding my body with chemicals that make me feel like I can fly.

One more whack to the ass literally has me screaming out loud.

"Yes, let it all out. Feel the orgasms I allow you to have. Over ... and over again."

His fingers don't stop touching me. My slit, my pussy, my clit. Twisting, turning, slipping, sliding. Everywhere. It's driving me insane.

Next thing I know, he shoves his cock into me.

All the way.

My lips part and an incredibly loud sighing moan slithers off my lips as he buries himself deep within me.

"Fuck ..." he whispers. "You're so fucking wet and open for me." He slaps my ass as he pulls out. "Perfect."

"Holy shit ..." I mutter, which makes him laugh.

He thrusts in again, this time even harder than before. "This pussy needed a good fucking, that's all. That's why you've been behaving so badly. You needed more of my cock, didn't you?"

"Yes ..." I cry out when he spanks me again. Fuck, I don't think I've ever felt this insane, this consumed by someone.

"Take it like a good girl then. Moan for me, Hailey. Let me hear how much you love this cock."

I moan for him, just like he asks. Not just because I love it, but also mostly because he tells me to.

Listening to him and letting him take charge gives me a release I haven't felt before.

Inner peace.

While being fucked like a whore.

Jesus Christ.

"Fuck yes," he growls, holding onto my ass while fucking me raw. "This is my pussy now. Tell me whose pussy this is, Hailey "

"Yours, Sir," I mewl.

"*My* pussy. And I will take this pussy how?"

"However you damn well please," I answer.

"Hmmm …" I can hear him smile. "Good girl. And you know what else? This pussy deserves all it gets."

"Yes, Sir. Please … fuck me."

"Are you that lusty, Hailey? So fucking turned on you'll beg me to claim you?"

"Yes, please, anything," I moan.

I don't even know what I'm saying.

What I'm thinking.

I'm numb, completely numb and void of any feelings other than pure, erotic need.

"This is what men fuck like, Hailey. And this man wants his pussy to come again," he growls. "Do it!"

WHACK!

The sound of his palm striking my ass reverberates through the room. With both hands, he grasps the ropes around my wrists and uses them as a handle to plunge in even deeper.

"Come. Now!"

The rim of his cock grinds against my sweet spot. My eyes almost roll back as my toes curl up, and the orgasmic waves engulf my body yet again. I struggle to breathe as he pounds me into the mattress; my muscles contract around his length, feeling every vein pulse with desire.

A loud howl, followed by a few thrusts, and he expels his seed into the condom inside me.

Panting, he releases himself and me. I sink down onto the bed, my body dropping sideways as I succumb to the intense energy drain. Fuck. Me. I could honestly fall asleep right now. That's how satiated I am.

Thomas pulls off the condom and ties a knot in it,

throwing it into the bin before he returns to me. With a satisfied look on his face, he sits down beside me on the bed and unties the rope around my wrists. I roll on my side as he goes to his cabinet again to take out some sort of cream, which he rubs all over my ass.

"For the pain," he says when I furrow my brows at him.

When he's done, I sit up straight and rub my lips while he cleans up all the stuff we used.

I don't know what to say. Everything feels awkward. Like we're hanging in the middle of something undefined.

"So ..." he mumbles, sitting down next to me.

"So ..." I repeat and look at him. "I guess it's not a good idea to be seen together."

He nods, staring at the wall. "For now."

"For now?" I say, smiling cheekily.

"Yeah. If we're going to do this more often, we have to be careful."

I grin, nodding too.

"You'd like that?" he asks.

"Yeah ... I think so."

His fingers curl around my chin, and he turns my head toward him. "But I want you to always remember I am still your teacher. If anyone asks, we never did anything, and we're not familiar with each other, other than being student and teacher. We didn't kiss. We didn't fuck. We never even touched."

"Gotcha." I make an arrow with my index finger and thumb and point it at him. "Well"—I get up from the bed—"I guess it's time for me to go then."

He just watches as I go back into the living room and collect all my clothes. It feels awkward with him leaning against the doorjamb. Somehow, he also managed to put on sweatpants while I wasn't looking. Too bad. I kinda liked staring at his dick.

Meow.

I scream.

"What the—" There's a cat running through my legs, almost making me fall. Jesus Christ. There's a cat. He has a cat?

Thomas laughs. "Ninja, don't scare her."

"You have a cat?" I say as if I didn't already see it with my own fucking eyes. "Why didn't I know that?"

Thomas laughs as Ninja hides under the bed. "He likes to hide when I have visitors. Doesn't like pussies he can't have."

Shaking my head, I laugh and slap my forehead. "You've got to be kidding me."

"What?" Thomas shrugs.

"That's gotta be one of the corniest jokes I've ever heard."

"Made you laugh."

I narrow my eyes at him but can't help smile. "That cat's probably just as much of a hermit as you are."

"Ha-ha. Very funny." He picks up Ninja and pets him. "Ninja and I just share a special bond."

"The bond of not getting laid enough," I retort.

"The bond of always attracting pussy wherever we go," he says. "I mean look what's in my house right this very moment."

"And you both have gigantic balls," I muse, watching him stroke the cat which raises its tail to expose some parts I'd rather not see.

"And proud of it," Thomas boasts.

I roll my eyes and stop fueling the fire by keeping my mouth shut. I put on my shoes and brush my fingers through my hair. Then I turn around. "So … I'll see you later then?"

"Um …" He points at my neck. "You put your dress on backward."

My eyes widen, and my cheeks turn red as I notice the little tag sitting just below my collarbone. How could I mess this up? Fuck, I'm stupid.

"The cat distracted me," I say.

He laughs as I hurry to take the dress off and on again, suddenly very conscious of the fact that I'm undressing in front of him. Again. I wonder if I'll ever get used to his penetrating gaze. It's like he fucks me with just his eyes. As if he still hasn't gotten enough. Will he ever?

Will I ever have enough?

So many questions I don't know the answer to.

All I know is that I don't want it to end … yet.

I bite my lip and say, "Um … Thanks. I guess. See you in class."

I turn around and walk toward the door when he interrupts me again. "Hailey … I'm going to make an appointment with the doctor for both of us. To get tested. I don't expect anything to show up, but I just want to make sure."

"Why?" I ask, my hand resting on the door handle.

"So I can fuck you bare. No condom."

That comment returns the heat to my body.

"I'll be expecting you to show up if you want this little thing we have to continue," he says.

I glance at him over my shoulder. "I'd like that."

His eyes narrow, but his tipping lip reveals a hidden smile. "Between the two of us … I don't think we could quit. Even if we wanted to."

I grin. "Touché." I turn around again but then hesitate. "Before I go … I just want you to know, I'm not some hooker you can just call up to get laid."

"Of course, not," he says.

"I have feelings too."

"I know," he says, taking a deep breath.

I lick my lips then ask, "Do you promise not to shove me aside again?"

His brows draw together, and he purses his lips. "I …"

"Don't tell me something you don't want to say," I interject. "I want the truth."

"I won't do it as easily as I did before," he says.

"You'd better not because I won't be as easy to win back either." I smile at him and then turn my head away, determined not to let him get to me.

Even though he already has.

Because who am I kidding? I'm already head over heels… and I know my crush is also doomed to fail.

But that doesn't mean a girl can't dream.

Right?

Chapter 16

Hailey

I come home in the middle of the night.

Lesley is fast asleep, snoring her way through what looks like raunchy dreams, judging by the amount of drool on her pillow. She moans a little when I close the door. I chuckle to myself as I take off my clothes and hop into bed. The moment my head touches the pillow, she groans again.

"You're back …" she mutters.

"Hmm. Just go to sleep."

"You were with him, weren't you?" Her voice suddenly sounds much more awake than usual.

I hesitate to answer, fearing the worst. "Yeah."

"Please tell me you're careful. And safe."

I thought she was gonna scold me. I didn't expect her to

actually worry. Not that she needs to, but it feels nice to know she cares so much.

I turn my head toward her. "Of course."

She smiles at me, but I can definitely see the troubled look she's trying to hide. "Don't let him hurt you."

"He'd never touch me that way," I reassure her.

"I mean your heart," she says. "He's your teacher, after all."

She's really worried about me, even though she doesn't need to be. But I understand. We're best friends after all, and best friends take care of each other. Even when one of them doesn't wanna hear it.

I nod. "I know."

She turns around and falls back to sleep again, but I'm still wide-awake.

My stomach churns with uncertainty.

She's right. He is my teacher. Is it wrong to fall for a guy like him? Is it doomed to fail?

I sigh and close my eyes.

Only one way to find out.

***

THOMAS

That night

I lie in bed, awake, unable to sleep.

I keep thinking about Hailey.

About our fun time together, and about how excited she makes me.

I smile to myself, wondering what she'll wear tomorrow. If I can make her blush with just a few words.

The color of her cheeks entices me.

But most of all, she provides me with a means to escape.

To fantasize and dream about something naughty and nice … instead of wallowing in my own misery.

Reluctantly, I close my eyes, hoping sleep comes soon so I don't have to lie awake all night as I often do. Hoping that, when it does finally come, it'll be gentle and smooth.

But I know that's only a lie I tell myself to fall asleep easier.

Tonight is no different.

In my dreams, it's morning, and I'm not in my apartment anymore. I'm in a place I used to call home. A place that's long gone, and now only exists in my memories.

The sun is shining brightly, a warm glow on my skin as I get out of bed. I walk into the living room and am greeted by the smell of buns roasting in the oven … or rather, burning.

Frowning, I check the stove. Black smoke fills the room as I open the door and take out the tray of burned buns, completely crisp and inedible. I throw the entire pan in the sink and cool it down while blowing away the smoke, and I open the windows to let it escape.

Strange.

Why would she put something in the oven and leave?

I call out her name, but there's no response.

I check all the other rooms, but she's nowhere to be found.

Until I come to the bathroom.

It's locked.

I knock. Three times. No response. I call out her name again. No response, even though I know she's in there.

Panic makes me shove my shoulder into the wood. Again and again, until it cracks and my muscles ache. When the lock breaks, I slam it open and rush into the bathroom ...

Only to find her resting in the tub.

Her head is underwater.

Her body is cold and white as snow.

I grab her body and pull her from the water, dragging her out of the tub and into my arms. My clothes are getting soaked, but none of that matters because all I can think of is how I can make her breathe.

I clasp my hands and press on her chest a few times, repeating the movement until suddenly she bursts into coughs. Water spills from her mouth. I breathe a sigh of relief and help her cough out the rest by holding her head so she doesn't swallow it back.

Tears well in my eyes at the sight of her.

Her eyes are watery. Empty. And the first thing that finally floods back into her isn't life. It's guilt.

Her hand lifts to meet my face, and I lean into her palm. Cradling her in my arms, I sniff and let the tears run. She's alive. She's here.

Still.

For now.

This is how it always goes.

How my dreams turn into nightmares and wake me up in the middle of the night, drenched in sweat.

But this time, I don't stop the dream.

I don't will it to end.

I just sit here in my dream world and let it all go.
Just like she did.

***

A few days later

During the day, I ignore whatever happened in my nightmares. I push them away into the deepest corner of my mind because I don't want to think about them. It's the only way I can stay sane.

What I *do* want to think about is that girl ... Hailey.

Every time I see her in class, I can't take my eyes off her.

Or my fucking filthy mind.

I imagine her naked in my bed, in my arms under the shower, fucking her in every way possible, showing her all the good in life. Sex. Lots of sex. I can't have enough.

I think she noticed too. She keeps smiling at me funnily, and I can't help smile back as if we're sharing a private joke. It always happens after I fuck her. It's like she knows I can't get enough of her.

I can't hide my attraction well.

God, I thought I knew what I was doing. That I was capable of keeping my feelings at bay, but I'm not.

Lately, I've been having these visions of us actually doing normal things. Like going to the movies, going out for dinner, or taking her on a fucking boat ride. Jesus, I've even thought of having a picnic and a fucking frolic in the grass. I don't fucking picnic or frolic.

But strangely, I'd do it for her, and I don't even fucking

know why.

In the dark, I fuck the girl who so desperately wants my attention.

But in the light ... I smile for her.

I want to see her happy.

For some reason, I want to get to know that girl I take home every now and then. That girl who hides her baggage behind vibrant clothes and bright red hair. It's as if she screams 'stay away from me,' but it only makes me want to come closer.

Something about her feels so familiar ... like something I can connect to.

And I rarely ever connect with anyone other than myself.

Or my cat.

No one comes close to my cat.

We have a connection on an otherworldly scale.

When class ends, all I wanna do is go over to her and kiss her, but that wouldn't be appropriate. All those other girls would get jealous of her, and we don't want that to happen.

So I text her on her cell, telling her to meet me at a park far away from the campus. I see her glance at me, a wicked smile forming on her face, and then she leaves. I go to her table and touch the wood, smelling my fingers afterward. I'm not crazy. I can actually smell her scent. Or maybe I am crazy. Addicted. Lost.

Or all of them at the same time.

This isn't good for her or me, but I can't stop.

So I go after her, to the place we agreed to meet.

I find her standing against a tree in the park that's rarely visited by students. A perfect place to meet unseen. Except for the fact that she's smoking.

She greets me with a smile, but I snatch the cigarette from her hand, throw it on the ground, and rub it out with my foot.

"Why'd you do that?" she snarls, placing her hand against her waistline.

"You shouldn't smoke," I say. "It's bad for you."

"Oh." Her hand drops, and she looks a bit befuddled. "Well, I'm not a kid. I can take care of myself."

"I can see that," I muse, raising a brow.

She sighs and rolls her eyes, but her lips still curl up into a tentative smile. I grab her chin and lift it gently, giving her a charming smile. "I don't want you to die early."

"Gee, thanks," she retorts.

"I mean it."

She licks her lips and looks down at the ground. "I know."

"Promise me you'll stop," I say, trying to get her to look at me by lowering my head to her level. "Don't smoke."

"I can't …"

"Do it for me?" I cock my head. "I'll give you a kiss every day you manage to keep it up."

I know it sounds corny, but it makes her laugh a little, so my job's accomplished.

"Fine."

"Good girl." I give her a quick peck on the forehead, making sure no one's looking.

She rubs her lips, her hair falling down her cheeks almost intentionally as if to cover a blush. A breeze makes her hair blow in my direction, and the sudden beauty in the movement enraptures me. Her pink, full lips and bright eyes draw my attention as she doesn't look anywhere but at me. In the light of day, she suddenly looks different. Less like the girl I fuck for pleasure and more like the girl I want to kiss for fun.

Almost instinctively, I lean in, my brain turning inactive from her sheer presence, and I smell the scent of her spicy perfume that reminds me of a tropical summer night at the beach in Hawaii. The energy she exudes washes over me just by being near her, and it fills me with something I haven't felt in a long, long time.

Something that makes me feel alive.

Her lips part and the moment I realize words are about to spill out, I press my lips to hers.

I don't want to interrupt her, but I couldn't stop myself either.

I just *had* to kiss her.

When the moment passes and our lips detach, I feel a sense of fulfillment that makes me smile.

I've clearly lost it this time.

Kissing a girl—no, not just any girl ... a student—in broad daylight in a place anyone could see us. If anyone's stupid, I am. I'm risking my career, and for what?

For what? For her.

For her.

Yes, for her.

I don't know why I'd say yes ... but for her, I'd do it.

Just the thought alone makes me pull back.

An uneasiness creeps onto her face, and I wonder why. Is it because I kissed her? Or because I'm *not* kissing her anymore?

"What's wrong?" I ask.

She shakes her head and smiles it off. "Nothing."

I frown and narrow my eyes. Something's up, but she won't tell me. I don't think it has to do with me, though. The way she looks into the distance and rubs her arms makes me think there's more going on in her life that I don't know about.

Of course, I don't.

I never asked.

Or ever gave the impression that I was interested.

I've been a fool.

How could I expect her to tell me when she knows it doesn't bother me enough to even ask? After all, I told her it was just sex ... and sex is really the best I can give her.

The only thing I shouldn't be giving her as her teacher, yet I don't want to stop either. In fact, every moment I spend with her only makes me want to pursue her further.

"So why'd you wanna meet up?" she asks, dragging me from my thoughts.

"Oh, right. Did you get your tests back?" I clear my throat.

"What tests?"

"From the doctor," I whisper, placing my hand on the tree next to her.

"Oh ... that." She makes it sound like it's some sort of despicable thing. "Yeah."

"And?"

She smirks and raises a brow at me, folding her arms. "You'd like to know, wouldn't you?"

I frown. "Oh, c'mon, Hailey. We don't have time for this bullshit."

"No, we don't have time to take it easy. You just wanna fuck me," she says. "Right?"

I sigh. "Just give me the damn answer."

"I will …" she muses, but I can already tell where this is going. "If you take me out on a date."

I take it back. I did *not* see this coming.

"You're not serious, right?"

She leans in. "As serious as you were when you told me to come to your apartment. *Now*." She tries to replicate my voice, which makes me cringe a little.

I take a deep breath.

She's got me in a corner now, and she knows it.

I want to fuck her, badly, every fucking day. It's all I can ever think about, and she knows it.

And now, she uses it against me.

"Smart little brat," I murmur.

She grins but doesn't respond, confirming my suspicions.

She's blackmailing me into going on a date with her.

"You're preventing me from fucking you without a condom unless I go out with you?"

"Uh-huh." She taps her foot. "I'm waiting." She checks her watch. "I have more classes today. Tick tock."

"Don't push me, Hailey."

"Do you wanna know or not?"

"Of course, I do," I growl.

"So you want to fuck me badly enough that you're considering it, but not badly enough that you'd take me out to dinner?"

"You don't know what I want," I say, putting my arm around her waist and pulling her close to me.

"Exactly my problem," she says, as if this was her plan all along.

Confuse me.

Until *I* don't even know what I want anymore.

I take another deep breath and close my eyes for a second. "All right."

"What?"

When I open my eyes, I see hers have widened.

"I'll do it," I say.

"Really?" She smiles and then hugs me. "Thank you."

At first, I'm overwhelmed, but when I let her warmth flow through me, I relax and wrap my arms around her.

Apparently, this means a great deal to her.

I'm honestly not sure why I agreed.

My dick was doing all the thinking.

Or maybe I really am starting to fall.

Fuck.

When she releases me, she says, "I know it's corny, but I just wanted us to go on a date. Like normal people, you know?"

"Hmm …" I narrow my eyes at her. "You do realize you're going to get spanked for this so hard, right?"

A shameless grin spreads across her lips. "I know, but I'll take the punishment like a good girl. After we get back from our first freaking date."

Chapter 17

THOMAS

A few days later

When I ring her bell, it's not her who opens the door to her dorm room but her roommate, and the look on her face, when she sees me, is anything but ecstatic.

"Oh … it's you." She sighs. "I thought they were coming to bring my package."

"Lesley, right?" I say, trying not to sound pompous.

"Yeah, that's me …" She clamps the door tight. "And you're the professor."

"Teacher," I correct. "Professor sounds so old."

"Right." She rolls her eyes. "What do you want?"

"I'm coming to pick up Hailey. Didn't she tell you we were going out?" I frown, placing my hand on the door too, so she won't slam it in my face.

"Uh ... no ..." She looks confused then turns her head. "Hailey!"

"Coming!" Her voice makes me smile.

"She'll be right there. Wait here." Lesley closes the door just a little and walks away.

There's enough of a hole left to peek through, and I can clearly see Hailey picking up some ice-cream cone earrings ... and completely forgetting to put away something else.

I grin as I watch her come to the door with a broad smile on her face. "Hi! Almost ready."

"Not quite," I say, pointing at her nightstand. "Is that the rabbit you were talking about?"

Her eyes widen, and her face turns beet red as she notices the pink dildo still lying next to her bed. "Shit."

She runs to it and quickly shoves it into a drawer, covering it with her body. "You didn't see anything."

I laugh. "Oh, yes I did ... you can bring it along sometime. I know just what to do with that."

"Oh, god." Lesley walks in with a look of complete disgust on her face. "Tell me I didn't just hear that." She puts her finger in her mouth and makes fake gagging noises.

"Just ignore us," Hailey says. "We'll be gone for the night, so you'll have the whole place to yourself."

"Please spare me the details!" Lesley says, making Hailey laugh.

Hailey comes toward me, and I ask, "You ready?"

"Not yet." She raises a brow and then wraps her arm around my neck, pulling me in for a kiss before I can lean back. She grins against my lips. "Now, I am."

"Fuck me. I need to bleach my eyes," Lesley growls,

groaning as she walks into the bathroom. "This is so awkward."

"Sorry!" Hailey says.

"Yeah, yeah, just go have fun, okay?"

"We will." Hailey grabs my hand and drags me with her.

I glance behind us to see Lesley catching another glimpse of us before closing the door.

"She doesn't like me, does she?"

"Who? Lesley?" Her forehead creases. "Nah, she's just a little worried about me, that's all."

I narrow my eyes. "Should she be?"

Hailey looks my way and then back at the floor again, shrugging. "I don't know. You tell me."

"She's just trying to protect you."

"From you, yeah," she muses, her laugh dying off quickly.

"Why? Do I look that dangerous?" I jest.

"Well … you're my teacher. I mean, she probably thinks I'm using you … or you're using me."

I lean in and whisper into her ear, "Or maybe we're using each other."

That makes her chuckle.

"She's right, you know," I say as we walk down the stairs. "I'm not the right guy."

"So what if she is? So what if you aren't? As long as it's fun …" The guilty look on her face only makes me want to stop and kiss her.

She knows just as well as I do that what we're doing is bad for us both.

But we can't stop.

It's exactly as she says. As long as it's fun. As long as it's distracting.

As long as …

How many more excuses can we have?

How many more can we make?

How many more until it's over?

"I'm excited," she says, pulling me from my thoughts. "I haven't been on a date in a long time."

"How long?" I ask.

"Maybe a year or something."

My pupils dilate. "A year? Jesus. And you still had boyfriends?"

"Yeah …" She scratches her head. "Wait, no, not really. Well, I did make out with a few boys at parties, and one did actually take me to a Burger King downtown."

"A Burger King …" I rub my face with the palm of my hand. "You've got to be kidding me."

"I wish. I'm a happy girl if a guy pays for my meal. One less bill to pay."

Fuck me.

Why would she accept just *that*?

Why doesn't she want more? More from a guy? More from me?

She deserves so much more.

I stop her in her tracks, grabbing her chin to make her look at me. "I'll do more than just pay your bills. I hope you realize that."

"I know … you'll also fuck me into oblivion."

Her comment makes me laugh as I release her from my grip. "That's not what I meant."

"Well, it's not like those boys knew what to do anyway. Why do you think I was still a virgin?"

I raise a brow. "Because you hadn't found the right guy yet. And now, you have."

Her lips part but they close again, and she seems a little lost with that statement.

I think I might've struck a chord there.

"C'mon," I say, opening the door for her. "Ladies first."

"Oh … such a gentleman," she says, passing me. "I almost believe it."

I slap her ass as I walk after her. "Only when I want you to."

And this time, I really want her to.

I don't know why, but I feel the urge to show her just how good I can be to her.

How I can be the guy she never had.

Or the guy she can never keep.

Sighing to myself, I open the passenger car door and let her slip into the seat before closing the door and walking over to the driver's seat. As I sit down and buckle up, I can't help but look at her in her short, green dress wearing her ice-cream cone earrings. I can't help but stare at her lips and that pretty pink shade on her cheeks. That awkward, closed-off girl who's playing with a strand of her red hair while staring off through the windows.

I wonder what she's thinking.
If it's the same as I am.

If she thinks I'm doing this only to get the results from the doctor back, or because of something more, something intangible.

If her heart is beating as fast as mine is, thinking about all the dirty things I want to say and do to her.

If she's secretly hoping I'll admit that I'm slowly falling

for her ... bit by impossible bit.

***

Hailey

As I look out the window, I notice we're not near the restaurant yet, even though we should've been there by now. When Thomas drives into an abandoned parking lot and stops, I turn around.

"Why are we stopping? This isn't the restaurant."

"Oh, I know, but I want to do something before we get there." He smiles in a way that makes goose bumps scatter across my body, even though he hasn't touched me yet.

"Do what?" I ask.

"Well, since you pretty much blackmailed me into taking you out, I figured I'd return the favor."

My eyes widen as he pulls out a metallic egg-like object that I recognize from the porn I've seen.

"You're going to wear this in your ass tonight."

"Oh, my god."

"Don't be scared," he murmurs. "It won't hurt ... much." The grin on his face makes me want to punch him.

"You tricked me."

"No, I didn't. I'm still taking you to the restaurant. I just want you to wear this while we're eating."

"A butt plug? Why?"

"Because I like it and because you'll do anything I say."

"I thought we were going to a restaurant."

"We are. I just want you plugged while eating." The smug look on his face makes my jaw drop.

"On a date?"

"On everything, really. Life's about enjoying, don't you think?" he muses. "I just like my enjoyment a little on the kinky side. That's all."

I sigh, rubbing my eyes with my fingers. "And here I thought we could have dinner like a normal couple."

He grabs my arm. "We're not a couple. And we're certainly not normal. Do you want to be? Do you want me to stop fucking you the way I do?"

I swallow away the lump in my throat. "No ... I think." Although I do think I'd want us to be a couple, I shouldn't be thinking that.

There's a stern look in his eyes. "You want me, you'll get me the way I am, and that includes my dirty fuckery, along with all the butt plugs and toys you can think of, everywhere and any place. I like my life spiced up, and I think you do too, more than you enjoy being normal. Whatever the fuck that is."

I take a deep breath and sigh. He's right. I just don't want him to be right. I don't wanna think that I'm fucked up.

"Fine," I say.

"You want dinner. I want those doctor's papers."

"And my painful ass," I add, which apparently makes him chuckle. "It's not funny."

"It is to me when you say it like that. You make it sound like a painful ass isn't a good thing, but you don't know that, do you? Have you ever been plugged before?"

"No," I say as I watch him grab some lube from the

back.

"Trust me when I say you'll love this."

I make a face. "I don't know …"

He raises his brow at me again, and it's the same look he always gives me when he wants something and won't take no for an answer. "I need you to wear this, Hailey."

"Why?"

"For my pleasure … and yours," he muses, as he pushes my arm until I twist. "Turn around."

"Do I really have to?"

"Yes. You didn't think I'd take you out to dinner without fucking you afterward, now did you?" he says. "Now, turn your ass toward me."

"But people—"

"No one's in the parking lot except for us, and if they do come, I have tinted windows, so no one can see a thing. Put your ass up, Hailey."

I reluctantly do as he says, his hand disappearing under my dress. He pulls down my panties, exposing my bare ass, and I look back when I hear the sound of the lube being squirted over the toy.

He glances at me while rubbing it around. "This'll feel cold, but you know that already. You've felt it before … but this time, it's a little bigger."

I gulp as he puts the tip close to my ass.

"Deep breath," he says.

When I do, he pushes it in, and all my senses explode, including the wordage from my mouth.

"Fuck! Shit! Holy shit! Fucking Jesus!"

He laughs. "I've never had that reaction before. Is it a good fuck or a bad fuck?"

"Uh, I don't know?!" I struggle to breathe as he inserts the plug into me. It feels so wrong, so dirty, so fucking full. Different from just a fucking finger. When it's in, he slaps my ass, making me jolt up and down from the pressure I feel. "Holy shit."

"Good girl," he says. "You should see your ass. It looks good on you. Crystal tip. A sparkling ass, just for me." He bites his lip, hissing a little as he rubs my ass. Then he clears his throat and pulls my panties back up again.

"Gotta control myself. First, it's time to eat food. Afterward, it's time to eat you."

I blush from that comment, but then the heat rushes through my body as I try to shift positions.

"Sit," he commands.

I try, slowly, but it feels so damn strange. When I'm finally on my ass again, I pull my dress down and try to compose myself, even though I feel indecent as fuck.

"How does it feel?" he asks.

"Um …"

"Are you aroused?"

Judging by the thumping between my legs, I guess that's a yes to the latter, so I nod.

A wicked smile spreads across his lips. "Good." He shifts the car into reverse and hits the gas. "Then we're off to have one lovely fucking dinner with a happy ending afterward."

Chapter 18

Hailey

Thirty minutes later

The restaurant is chic as fuck. Seriously, I'm not kidding. I've never been to a place like this. It has tablecloths, different glasses for wine and water, two of every cutlery, and they talk to me as if I'm some kind of lady from the middle ages. Waiters here walk as if they just shit gold glitter from their ass.

It's terrifying, to say the least.

But I have to admit the food is beyond delicious.

Every time I take a bite of my venison tenderloin, I die a little. That's how good it is. And maybe a moan or two even slips out.

Thomas keeps looking at me with a stupid smile on his

face, and I constantly have the feeling that I'm being laughed at for using the wrong fork and knife, but I don't care.

"How is it?" Thomas asks.

"Delicious!" I say.

He chuckles. "I can tell from the moans."

"Sorry ... I just can't control myself."

He leans forward, whispering, "Or is it the plug?"

I almost choke on a little venison there but manage to swallow it down eventually. "I'm trying not to pay attention to it."

"Oh, so me talking about it only makes you feel it more? Nice to know." He grins.

"Stop it," I hiss.

"Why? Am I embarrassing you?"

"Yes. It feels wrong here."

"Here? Is this place any different from college? I could do this anywhere," he muses, taking a bite of his crab.

"If I knew you were taking me to such an uptight place, I would've dressed nicer."

"You look amazing, Hailey," he says, making me blush.

I rub my earlobes, only to be reminded of those earrings I put in. I love them, but wearing them to something this fancy is really awkward. "Well, I just feel so out of place here with my ice-cream cone earrings."

"Hmm ..." He licks his lips. "They only make you more beautiful."

I try to hide my smile behind my fork, but it doesn't work. Luckily, he smiles back. Compliments ... why do I fall so damn hard for them every goddamn time?

"You're uncomfortable," he says.

"No, not at all," I say, clearing my throat, but he knows as well as I do that I'm lying.

"I won't hide my opinion of you, Hailey. I'll tell you whatever's on my mind. Bad or good. You okay with that?"

"Yeah, why wouldn't I be?"

He shrugs. "Some people can't take the heat."

"I think I've already proven I can." A self-satisfied smile perks up on my face.

"All right ... then let's continue our game. Ask three questions and I'll answer them, then you do the same."

"You wanna play a game again? I thought we were already over this," I say.

"There's plenty more I can learn about you. We're only just about to get to know each other," he says, taking a sip of his wine.

I purse my lips. "So you *do* want to get to know me beyond the bedroom?"

It takes him a while to put down his wine glass and think of an answer. "I want to know who I'm fucking ... literally." He leans forward. "So what's it going to be, Hailey? Will you allow me to get to know your mind as well as I know your body?"

"Assuming you know my body so well ... maybe I will," I say, taking a sip of my drink. "All right, you start."

He sits back in his chair, mulling it over a bit. "Would you have come to class and done better if I wasn't teaching?"

I make a face. "What kind of question is that?"

He shakes his finger. "Ah-ah. Answer first. Question later."

I roll my eyes. "Fine. I don't know. Maybe I would have.

But I'm not skipping any of your classes now, am I?"

"But you did," he taunts, tracing an invisible line on the table.

"My turn. Would you ever have remotely thought of fucking me if you'd never met me before our first class?"

"Absolutely." He smirks. "Attraction would've happened, whether I met you before or later. Would I have acted on it? Probably not. But that's not the way it went with us, now did it? We can take so many paths in life, but there's no use thinking about them because we chose only one. That's the one we should believe in. It's all we can do. Believe we made the right choice."

I nod. There's actually a lot of wisdom behind that statement. "True. As long as you stand behind the choice."

"I don't know about you, but I don't even want to know what would've happened if we didn't meet."

Everything he says makes me feel like I should be trying my best more. He seems so much more interested and actually okay with the choice he made when he fucked me. It's almost like he's finally coming to terms with our 'relationship.' Or whatever the fuck this is we're doing.

"So ... second question ... Where did you get those earrings?"

My eyes widen. "Excuse me?"

"Where'd you get those?" He points at them, and my instinct is to immediately grab them and hold on tight.

"What does it matter?"

He shrugs. "It doesn't if they wouldn't matter to you, but they do."

My words stick in my throat. "H-how do you know?"

He smiles. "C'mon now, Hailey ... this isn't the first

time we met, and I'm starting to recognize your little quirks. It's not a shame that they mean a lot to you. I'm just curious."

I sigh and turn my head toward the table so I can think about it for a second. It's none of his business. Or is it? Does he mean something to me? Enough to tell him more about me? Do I mean enough to him that he'd want to know? Apparently.

Taking a deep breath, I say, "I got them from my father for my seventh birthday. I know they're stupid, and I'm too old to wear them, but I love them."

He lowers his head and nods, then looks up with a cocked head and a smile. "I get it. Your dad means a lot to you, and that's truly admirable. I hope he loves you just as much."

I rub my lips together, biting the bottom one in the process. "I hope so." My throat suddenly feels tight, and I can't swallow well, so I quickly take a sip of my drink and say, "Next question. Will we ever be more than fuck buddies?"

His lips part, but then he slams them shut again, a difficult look on his face. "You know I can't answer that question, Hailey."

"You can't, or you don't want to?"

He just looks at me without saying a word.

I shrug it off. "It was worth a shot." Honestly, I am a little bit disappointed and hurt. I mean, he could've just said no, right? No hard feelings. Or something.

I sigh in my head. Who am I kidding? Of course, there are hard feelings. I don't just fuck any guy. In fact, I never fucked a guy before him, and that means something to me.

It may not mean something to him, but at least, he could acknowledge the fact that I'm here and I'm not going anywhere.

"I want to know about your dreams, Hailey," he says. "What do you want to do after college?"

"My dreams?" I frown, confused. "I hadn't thought about that yet."

"What would you see yourself doing in ten years from now?"

"I don't know. Maybe start up a business somewhere." I clear my throat. "But you haven't answered my question yet."

"I don't want to. Can't we talk more about your parents? Or your hobbies? I'd like to know more about you," he says.

"I don't wanna talk about my parents. Anything but my parents." I put the glass down a little too hard, making the wine splash over and onto my shirt. "Fuck."

He picks up a napkin and leans over the table. "Damn, let me help you."

He pats my shirt, but I snatch it away from him and dab my clothes myself. "I have hands. I can clean myself. Thanks."

"No problem. Also, we don't have to talk about your parents. Just tell me something else."

I throw the dirty napkin on the table. "What's there to tell? I'm a unicorns-and-rainbows-loving nerd, who prefers loud music over talking to people, who also happens to love bright colors and anything that distracts her. I'm pretty weird, but also pretty normal. Did I mention I love to party and hang out with boys?" I raise a brow to taunt him.

"As long as those boys don't touch you, party away."

"Really?" I shift in my seat. "Because I could've sworn I wasn't anyone's possession, so boys can touch me all they want, and I'll gladly let them if they want to."

He narrows his eyes. "Don't play dirty games with me, Hailey. I'm not someone to mess with."

"Oh, and I am?"

"Why are you so upset? Is it because I asked about your parents? That's it, right?"

My nose twitches from annoyance. He's really pushing me now.

"Or is it because I never said you're mine?"

He reaches into his pocket.

Something inside starts to vibrate.

I squeal.

Everyone turns around.

Thomas places his finger on his own lips and shushes me.

"Don't make a sound."

"What the fuck?" I say.

"Shh ... not so loud. You don't want everyone here to know you have a butt plug in your ass, do you?" he whispers.

"Is that thing vibrating? Oh, my god." My pupils dilate and then I growl, "*You're* doing this."

"Yes, I am. I needed to make a point here."

"What point?" I shudder and clench my legs from the vibration, which pulses through me, causing delicious thumps.

Fuck. How am I supposed to concentrate on the conversation? How am I supposed to eat my damn venison if I can't lift a damn fork without shaking?

"You are mine, Hailey. Whether you think you are or not doesn't matter. When I say you're mine, you're mine completely. No one, and I mean no one, is going to touch you. I don't share what belongs to me."

"I don't belong—"

"You belonged to me the moment I stuck my tongue into your pussy, and you know it," he growls softly. "You think I'm playing around, don't you? I'm not. I may not want to define whatever the fuck it is we're doing here, but that doesn't make me any less of a greedy motherfucker. And I am *fucking* greedy when it comes to you. That's a problem of mine that I'm willing to admit now, having you on my mind every goddamn second of the day, wishing I could stick my tongue in your pussy and then my cock until I hear you scream my name. I also finally came to terms with the fact that I am one jealous asshole, and you won't like me one bit when I'm jealous, Hailey, so don't you make me one by letting other boys get a taste."

I'm baffled.

I don't even know what to say.

Completely fucking speechless, that's what.

And I don't even know if I'm supposed to take this as a compliment or a threat.

Judging by the sensations between my legs, I guess it's good either way.

Not that I still have a choice in the matter. The more he talks, the more I want him to shut up and kiss me.

Now, I know what Lesley means when she's talking about alpha men. He's the prime example.

"Did you understand all that, Hailey?"

"Um ... yes? I guess?" I say, licking my lips from the

tightness in my ass that I'm suddenly very aware of, considering we're in a restaurant.

The vibrating increases in intensity, making me squirm in my seat.

"Not. Good. Enough," he growls. "Tell me exactly what you won't be doing."

"I won't be seducing guys or letting anyone else touch me."

"And?"

"I belong to you, even though we aren't boyfriend and girlfriend."

"Exactly. And when I ask you to tell me something, you *will* tell me."

"Fine, yes," I whisper, breathing heavily through my mouth to cope with the increased pleasure I'm feeling down below. Goddamn. It feels so wrong inside a restaurant.

"Yes, what?" He pulls the item from his pocket and shows it to me. "Or do you want me to turn this up a notch?"

"Yes, Sir!" I say, a little bit louder than intended, causing people to turn their heads.

He smiles wickedly. "Good."

The vibrating loses its power, but it doesn't stop completely.

"Why are you doing this?" I mutter. "We're in a fucking restaurant."

"I don't care where we are. I will give you pleasure whenever I want, wherever I want. Because… let's face it, that wasn't really punishment, was it? Tell me the truth." he muses, placing the item on the table in full view. Goddamn, it feels like a jab. Like he knows he owns me or something.

Of course, he does. I know it too. I just wish I could own him too.

I sigh and pat my dress, trying to regain whatever's left of my self-control. "Yes, Sir ... I kinda liked it."

"Hmm ... that's my good girl."

Just those words ... they do something to me.

Especially the part when he says 'my.'

It makes my stomach flutter.

Thomas picks up his fork and takes a few more bites before putting it down again. Then he looks at me, at my plate, my fork, and points. "Are you done?"

I nod, trying to act as normal as possible while my ass feels like it's on fire.

"Then let's get outta here."

"But we haven't had dessert yet."

"Oh ... I know." He grins. "We'll get to that part soon." He casually waves at the waiter. "Bill please!"

Chapter 19

THOMAS

On the way back to my place, I grab her hand and place it on my dick. It instantly stiffens from her touch, and I guide her along the shaft until she gets the picture. "Don't be gentle," I say, licking my lips. "Get it nice and warmed up. When these pants come off, I want to be ready to bury myself deep inside you."

She sucks in what seems like a sultry breath and licks her lips too. "You haven't told me what we're going to do yet …"

"You'll know soon enough. I like the element of surprise, especially when I use it on a girl like you."

"A girl like me? Tell me, what kind of girl am I?" she purrs, stroking me harder.

I grin as I hit the gas even harder. "Quirky. Insecure. Inexperienced. Willing. Needy. And above all … so damn sexy when you're spunky."

"Insecure? I think you have the wrong girl. Does it feel like I am?" She squeezes my length and then pulls down my zipper, taking out my cock from my underpants.

"Fuck … maybe I underestimated you." I moan as she begins to rub me.

She smiles and spits into her hand, then slathers it all over my rock-hard cock. Fuck me. She's jerking me off with both hands now, and I'm trying to drive.

"I might not have had a lot of boyfriends, but that doesn't mean I never saw a dick. It also doesn't mean I never did anything with them."

"Who, boys?"

"Dicks."

I laugh but then my laugh quickly subsides as she hits a sweet spot.

"Plus I've learned a thing or two from my horny roommate. That and porn."

"What else have you learned from porn?" I ask, biting my lip. "Just curious."

She raises a brow. "I'll show you."

She bends over and suddenly her head is between my legs. When her tongue touches my base, I almost explode.

"F-Fuck …" I try to hit the brakes because I'm going too fast after what she just did, but it's fucking hard to use your leg when you're being sucked off.

Her mouth is so soft and wet, and her tongue feels so good against my skin. I can tell from the way she's licking me that she's really getting into it. I'm honestly starting to think she's done it before. Maybe not as virginal as she described.

"Not your first rodeo, is it?" I murmur.

"No, but don't you deny you love it," she says between sucks.

"Oh, I would never," I moan. "Fuck, but you did lie a little about you being a virgin."

"No cock in my pussy before you means I'm a virgin. At least, it does to me."

"Funny," I say. "You're a naughty little girl, aren't you?"

"Are you gonna let me suck you off, or are we gonna talk?" she asks, raising her head.

My brows furrow, and I place one hand on top of her head. "Suck. Talk later."

She smiles as I push her head down onto my lap. Fuck, that feels good. So good, I don't even care about the speed limit anymore. I'm a bad, bad teacher … and right now, I honestly don't give a fuck.

I just want her.

That's all.

When we reach my home, I park the car. She raises her head, exposing my saliva-covered dick, which bounces up and down from the sight of her red, swollen lips.

"We there already?"

"Yes," I say, putting my cock back into my pants and zipping up again.

"Aw, I was just enjoying that."

"Won't be your last time either," I say as I turn toward her. "Now … the papers."

"Papers?" She looks confused. "Oh, right, you mean the doctor's." She rummages in her purse and takes out a paper, showing it to me. "Here."

I take it from her hands and quickly scan through it. A smile slithers onto my face. Fuck yes.

"And you?"

"I'm clean," I say. "Please tell me you're on the pill."

"Of course, I am," she affirms.

"Good," I say, handing her back the paper. "And since you are clean too, that means we can fuck like real rabbits."

She grins, and I get out of the car and close the door. I walk around the car and open the door to help her out. Well, help, as in grabbing her hand and dragging her with me into my apartment building like the caveman I can sometimes be. It literally takes all my fucking effort not to grope her in the elevator, but I don't want our sexcapades caught on tape, and since there's a camera in this little tiny metal box we're in ... well, you get the picture.

Suffice to say, once we reach my door, I immediately smash my mouth into hers.

"Fuck, you sucked me so good. You almost made me come," I groan into her mouth.

"Almost? More like damn-we-didn't-have-enough-time."

"I was on the verge of bursting multiple times. I would've come in your mouth if I wasn't too busy trying to get us home alive."

She laughs. "Right ... I'm not that good."

I bite my lip and press another soft, sensual kiss on the right side of her mouth. "It was so good. I'm going to make you do it again."

"Now?"

"I already had other plans for you tonight, but now that I know how good you are with your tongue, I'm going to make you use it more often. And the next time, you won't be the one deciding the pace."

"Oh ..." She grins, chuckling devilishly. "Continue ..."

I lean in, grab her by the waist, and whisper into her ear, "Next time you suck me off, it's going to be rough, and I might come in your throat, depending on whether I can choose between filling your mouth or your ass."

She closes her eyes and she hisses; the sound so familiar it makes my cock twitch again. She makes that sound when her panties are soaked from just my words. The effect I have on her is amazing. We're attuned to each other, like we can feel each other's needs without even having to say a word.

Connected in a different way.

Connected, not just with sex ... but something deeper.

But now is not the time to explore that.

My cock is too hard and eager, and the heat in her pussy is begging to be quenched.

My hand drifts to her dress, and I casually slide down her zipper, peeling away the dress. It falls down onto the floor, our eyes never ceasing contact. The silence between us is electrifying, so much so, that I immediately pull away the clip that keeps her bra in place and let it fall too. Her panties are gone within a few seconds too.

Without lowering my head, I let my eyes roam free across her body, taking in her perfect figure, with its dimples and blemishes, admiring each and every one of them.

From top to bottom and back again. Her face, framed by a bob cut, so sweet and innocent, with a smile that could warm even the most frozen of hearts.

A heart like mine.

I take a fistful of her hair and pull, forcing her head

down as my lips smash to hers. I push and push until she goes to her knees, at which point our lips detach. Her tongue dips out to wet them, almost as if she's begging for more without actually asking for it, and I oblige.

I reach down for her chin, tilt her head, and kiss her once more before turning away.

"Wait here," I say.

She doesn't even object.

The soundlessness of her non-existent protest is like music to my ears.

Even though just minutes ago we were having what seemed like an argument, it's now turned into the greatest bliss there is.

Sex without repercussions. Sex without guilt.

Just sex.

And maybe a little bit of heart.

Just a tiny bit.

So tiny, it's practically invisible.

And if anyone asks, I'll deny it's there ... even though it is.

Chapter 20

Hailey

I sit on my knees on his floor, awaiting his return. I don't move from my spot. I don't ask questions. I do what a good girl does … wait for her lover to return.

I don't feel like I need to move or say anything. I'm content where I am now.

Well, apart from the buzzing in my ass, but now that I've felt it for so long, I've almost gotten used to it. Every jolt reminds me of him and how he steals my breath away.

I'm addicted to him.

Addicted to giving myself away to someone like him, someone I can feel in my heart I can trust.

Addicted to the power play.

The distraction.

The sex.

Because that's all it is.

God, I'm a liar, but a good one too.

When I feel his hand on my shoulder, I melt a little.

He said I belonged to him. That he owned me. That I'm his.

And those words went straight to my head.

Made me so complacent and weak in the knees.

"Hands behind your back," he says, and I do just that. Something soft and silky is tied around my wrists. "I'm going to put something over your eyes too. Don't be alarmed."

He holds a dark, purple scarf in front of my head, and brings it closer until it blocks out the light, binding it around my head. It smells like him, and I imagine him wearing this under a thick coat in the winter.

"Stand up," he says, and I get up from my knees.

I hear him circle around me, a soft, leathery sound in the background. My ears focus on the sounds more now that I can't see, and I can hear every breath he inhales and every thump of my heart in my throat.

His fingers twist around my neck, and a warm, wet kiss is placed on my collarbone. Then my neck. And another one just below my ear. "Are you mine?"

"Yes, Sir," I whisper as his tongue dips out to lick my earlobe.

His hand suddenly cups my pussy, making me jolt. "Is this pussy mine and mine alone?"

"Yes, Sir," I whimper as he rubs his fingers up and down.

He swats my pussy softly, but enough to make me

squirm. "Spread your legs."

I do what he says as I feel his hand drift up and down my body, toying with my senses. His lips disappear from my neck only to reappear on my nipples, nibbling and sucking gently. His fingers between my legs make me wet and weak in the knees.

"What will you do for me?" he asks.

"Anything you desire, Sir," I respond.

I know it makes him hard.

And it makes me so goddamn wet when he does what he wants.

We're a match made in heaven.

"Exactly." He grasps my ass and smacks one cheek so hard my body almost tips forward. Just that single hand on my belly keeps me in place. "My ass. My pussy. My fucking girl," he growls, making me wanna swoon.

Suddenly, his hands disappear, and then I feel his hot breath on my pussy lips. Next thing I know, his tongue is on my clit, swirling around, making me all hot and bothered. I struggle to stay standing and stop my legs from quaking. His mouth is just that good. He knows exactly what to do and where to go. How to get me to moan. How to get me to beg.

"Fuck ..." I whimper.

"Fuck? Is that a question, Hailey?" he growls, slapping my ass, which only makes my body push into his mouth more. "Tell me."

"Fuck, yes, please."

"What? What do you want me to do to you?" he asks.

"Fuck me, please, Sir."

"How?" His voice is stern but sexy.

"Anywhere, anyway. Just give it to me."

"Hmm … with my tongue?" He sucks on my clit so hard it makes me moan out loud.

"Or with my finger?" He pushes a finger into my pussy, making me fully aware of the fact that the plug is still in my ass. It gives so much pleasure that I'm about to burst.

"Fuck, I wanna come so badly."

His finger slips out, and his tongue disappears. "Not yet, Hailey." I groan, and he slaps me again. "No growling at me. You'll take whatever I give, and believe me, you'll want that."

He takes a fistful of my hair and pushes my head down while pulling his zipper down. I already know what's gonna happen next.

"Open your mouth."

I do what he says, and he shoves his cock into my mouth. "Get it nice and wet."

Pre-cum coats my tongue as I struggle to lick him while he holds me. I try not to push back, but he can't go too far either. I'm not used to this yet, although I'm really starting to like it. My clit keeps thumping every time I taste him, and it makes me wanna go all the way.

But then he pulls himself out of my mouth again. "On the floor."

I sink to my knees, but he pushes my head down even further. "Lower. Head on the floor."

My ass is high in the air in order to stay facedown on the floor, and I think that's exactly what he wants. I can feel his hands slide across my body to my ass, where he positions himself.

"This might be a little uncomfortable … but you'll love

what comes next."

He tugs at the plug, slowly pulling it out. It hurts a little, but when it's out, I let out a sigh of relief. It wasn't that hard.

"I'm going to fuck you now. No condom. No holds barred. First, I'm taking your pussy. Then your ass." His hard-on pokes against my entrance. "And you're going to like every fucking thrust I give you."

I moan out loud when he enters my pussy from behind, not giving me a second to adjust. He immediately starts pounding into me, fucking me like a wild animal. My tongue darts out to wet my lips, but I can't seem to pull it back in. I feel like a goddamn whore, wasted on lust, and I don't give a damn.

He thrusts and thrusts until sweat drips down my back and my cheeks burn. My pussy clenches around his cock, desperate to come, desperate for more. When I'm at my limit and sucking in the breaths, he pulls out.

Only to squirt something cold and wet on my ass.

And then push his tip against my ass.

"Remember how the plug felt? This is the same, only different. Bigger. Fuller. Longer." He pushes in, and I hold my breath. "Harder."

A tiny cry escapes my mouth as he enters me, my hole feeling so tight around his thickness.

"Take it like a good girl, Hailey, and I'll let you come. Would you like that?"

"Yes, Sir," I moan, as he pushes in farther.

"Almost there …" He groans, his cock feeling so big inside me that it almost makes me think it won't fit. When he reaches the base, his hand settles on my ass, and he says,

"Good … Now, tell me if it hurts and I'll stop, but don't call out if it's not needed. You'll feel full, but it'll feel good after a while, and then you'll want nothing less, trust me."

"Yes, Sir," I say, taking in a small breath.

But it doesn't prepare me for when he starts to move.

Slowly, he pulls out and pushes into me, my ass feeling like it's being pounded, even though he moves so little. It feels just like the plug, only much bigger, and the sensation makes me feel like I could explode. That could also be my pussy, though, as the tension makes my clit thump even harder than before.

"Oh, your ass feels so good around my cock, Hailey." He thrusts in and out, his fingers gripping my skin, nails digging in.

I bite my lip and move along with him as the pleasure increases. Soon, I'm used to the fullness of having him inside me, and I moan along with him. "F-Fuck …"

"Hmm … that good, huh?" he muses, and he grabs the tie around my wrists. "I should've claimed your ass sooner."

He uses the tie as reins, slamming into me from behind so hard my face rubs along the carpet. I feel dirty, but I love every nasty second of it.

One of his fingers dives between my legs, and he starts toying with my pussy. "Oh damn, you're so wet." A growl-chuckle escapes from his mouth. "You filthy little girl. I'm gonna fill your ass to the brim with my cum."

He flicks my clit until I'm panting, hot-feverish sweat dripping down my back as I'm dying to come. My whole body shakes with desire and need, and my brain has turned to mush.

"Come for me," he growls. "Come. Now!"

His fingers and his voice are all I need to fall apart. Right there, with his cock buried deep inside me. My moan doesn't even come close to his as he thrusts a final time. The warm gush of his seed spilling into me feels like bliss, and I come so hard from just the idea, I almost faint. That's how good it is.

"Fuck …" He groans, shoving his length into me a few more times, his cum still shooting into my ass. The longer he goes on, the slower he goes, until he pulls out and his dick grows flaccid against my skin. My breath is ragged, and we're both panting as he pulls at the tie and drags my body up toward his.

"God …" he murmurs, untying the cloth around my head. "You undo me."

When the light reappears, I blink a couple of times, still dizzy from the roughness and sweet bliss.

He unties my wrists, and I almost collapse on the floor, but he holds me tight to his body.

"Steady …" he whispers in my ear, his hands wrapped around my waist. "You did so well." I hear him sniff close to my hair, and then press a soft kiss against my neck.

I lean back into his embrace, tired and completely consumed by his lust.

He places one hand under my knee and the other under my armpit and lifts me as he stands up. I gasp, sucking in the much-needed air as he carries me into the bathroom.

"What are you doing?" I ask.

"I fucked you pretty roughly … And now, it's time for me to take care of you."

"Why?" I mutter, still a bit heady. "I can take care of myself. I know how a shower works."

He places me under the showerhead and turns it on, letting the water stream down on us both. "I know you do, but just because you can doesn't mean you should. Sometimes, you need to let yourself get pampered."

I smile and shake my head as he grabs a bit of gel, rubs his hands together, and then starts lathering it all over my body.

"I can wash myself," I say, looking him directly in the eye as his hands run over my breasts.

"I know. But I want to do this." He grabs my wrist when I attempt to take the bottle from him. "Let *me* do this."

His words shut me up all right.

Not because of the sternness in his voice but because of the underlying consideration.

He doesn't just wanna fuck me until he's satisfied. He's gotten to a point where he wants to take care of me. Make me feel good.

I stop fighting him. Stop resisting his domineering behavior.

I stop because there's no reason anymore.

No reason to deny the fact that I'm totally and utterly falling in love with this man.

This man ... my professor. My teacher.

When we're finished showering, he even dries me off with a towel, taking extra care to be gentle on my sore bits. He knows exactly where it hurts just by glancing at my face whenever he passes a certain spot. He's diligent, almost as if he's petting something precious to him, and I can't help but smile at him each time he looks at me.

We go back into the living room, and I gather my

clothes off the floor while he throws his in the washing bin. I attempt to put my clothes back on, but then I hear his voice right behind me. "What are you doing?"

"What does it look like?" I say. "Putting on my clothes so I can go home. You don't expect me to walk back naked, do you? That'd be cruel. I mean, I'll do a lot of things for you, but my answer to that would be fuck you."

He laughs and wraps his hand around my waist, pulling me in for a soft kiss right underneath my ear. "Relax. I'm not asking you to do anything ... except stay."

I suck in a breath.

Stay.

Did he just say that out loud or was I fantasizing?

He walks in front of me, grabbing my hand and guiding me toward his bedroom. I stumble behind him, feeling like a lost sheep as he takes me to his bed. I don't refuse as he pulls me closer and sits down on his bed, pulling me onto his lap. All I can do is stare at his beautiful eyes as he pulls me down on the bed with him. My head rests on his chest and his hand on my back. Our naked bodies aligning, our breathing synchronized. The darkness and silence in the room take over, but it doesn't make me feel alone or afraid.

I have the sound of his heartbeat filling me with warmth and his scent to keep me company, and at that moment, for just a few seconds, I don't feel like we're student and teacher anymore.

"What does this mean?" I ask, breaking the silence.

"What?"

"Us ..."

He turns his head toward me, his fingers still gently thrumming my skin. "You mean us lying in bed together?"

I smile and trail my fingers along his chest. "That too … I mean, you've never invited me to stay."

"Never?" He ponders it over. "Hmmm … Well, there's a first time for everything."

"I know. I just wonder what it means. Like, what does *this* mean? Us, together." I really don't know how to word it without sounding like an obsessive girlfriend. Or without scaring him to the point of chasing me away.

His brows draw together, and his lips turn to thin lines. "Nothing. It's just sex. And now, we're going to sleep." He turns on his side, away from me.

"Nothing," I repeat, mulling it over a bit. After a while, I ask, "Is that what you want?"

He glances at me over his shoulder. "Maybe."

"Maybe?" I give him a stupid face. "Is that all you're gonna say?"

"You're not easily satisfied, are you?" he says.

"No," I say, shrugging and laughing it off.

"Well, that's as much as you're going to get from me for now."

"For now …" I say. I like that word.

I like for now and maybe. They're better than no and never.

"How many times are you going to repeat my words?" he muses.

I stare up at the ceiling. "As many times as needed to get the point across."

Now, he turns to face the ceiling too. Totally not awkward or anything. "And what point is that?"

"The point that we're in limbo and I don't know what to think of it."

"I like limbo," he says, a smug smile on his face as he gazes at me.

"I don't," I say, folding my hands.

He sighs and closes his eyes. "Let's just get some rest, okay?"

"I'm not tired."

"Well, I am. It's late, and we've done a lot of ... physical exercise."

I laugh at those words. He goes through so much trouble just to avoid the topic, it's funny.

"I think I like you more than just for the sex," I blurt out.

I didn't mean to, it just slipped out of me because it's been on the tip of my tongue for a while now.

Fuck.

Now, I feel embarrassed.

Why did I have to say that out loud?

And in such a stupid way?

When he doesn't respond, I breathe a soft sigh of relief, glad he didn't hear it.

Maybe he was already asleep.

"Good night, Hailey."

Fuck.

So he did hear it.

He just doesn't wanna reply.

My heart sinks to a new all-time low, and I suddenly feel cold to the bone. I turn away from him and tuck my head deep into the pillow, trying not to make a noise as I slam my face into it, wishing I'd never opened my mouth. I ruined a great evening. No, screw that, I ruined whatever good thing we had. I grab the covers and pull them up to my neck, hoping he'll fall asleep soon so I can squirm out and get away before things get more awkward the next morning.

I didn't take into account that he'd turn around, wrap his arms around my waist, and pull me closer to him. And I certainly didn't expect him to nuzzle me, peck me on the back, and hug me tight. Like a real boyfriend would.

With only just a small detail missing.

He's not my boyfriend ... But we'll get to that part later.

At least, that's what I tell myself as I snuggle deeper into him and let his breathing lull me to sleep. It's heaven, sleeping next to him.

Until he wakes up screaming his lungs out.

Chapter 21

THOMAS

Her tears and defeated face are the only things on my mind as I hear her speak. She's not happy. She's not feeling good. Everything is wrong, including me ... including her.

It's just like before, only worse.

Shreds of memories fly past.

Her, screaming at me.

Her, crying in a corner.

Her, not getting out of bed until late at night.

Her tear-stained face and that endless smile that permanently marked her face when I saw her below my window.

So beautiful.

So much ruin.

My lungs break with noise that I can only describe as screeching.

A desperate attempt to breathe while suffocating on misery.

That's when I wake up.

Sweat rolls down my back and forehead, and I jump out of bed like a ghost is haunting me. I turn on the light and look around. It's then that I notice the girl in my bed. Hailey.

She looks at me, blanket pulled up to her shoulders, her eyes scared.

"Oh, god ..." I murmur. "Did I hurt you?"

She shakes her head. "You were yelling. What's wrong?"

I swallow and push back the lump in my throat. "Nothing." I turn around and walk into the living room, immediately checking that the oven is off. Then I close all the windows and check the bathroom to make sure none of the faucets are dripping.

As I turn around, I come face to face with Hailey.

"You're acting strange." She folds her arms. "Tell me what's wrong."

I frown. "I'm fine; go back to bed."

When I try to pass her, she places her hand on the wall next to me. "Not without you."

"I'll be there in a minute. Just go on ahead," I say, but she's not listening.

She narrows her eyes at me. "Something's wrong. You wake up screaming, and you go check every damn thing in the house?"

I sigh. "It's nothing. Just let it go."

I push past her, but she still opens her mouth. "It's something you're not letting go. You just don't wanna tell me."

I go to my kitchen and take a bottle of whiskey from the

cabinets, then pour myself a much-needed drink.

"Drinking? In the middle of the night?" She comes closer and raises her brow at me, gazing at me with a judging look.

"What?" I say, holding the glass. "It's my house. I can have a drink when I want."

She picks up the bottle and grabs another glass. "Fine. Then I'm drinking too."

I place the glass down on the table. "You can't do that."

"Why not? You're drinking too." She picks up the glass and holds it close to her mouth.

"Stop."

She pauses, her eyes darting to me.

"If I stop, you stop," she says. "You told me I should quit smoking. Well, you should quit drinking."

I frown. "I don't have a problem."

"Oh, really? Then what are you doing with two bottles of whiskey and rum?" She points at my trashcan, which contains more bottles.

Fuck. She caught me.

Sighing out loud, I turn around and growl at the sink. Then I throw the contents of my glass down the drain. Goddammit. Why does she always have to do that? Why does she always manage to puncture me and go right to my soul?

"What did you see?" she asks.

"What?"

Suddenly, she's behind me, and she places her hand on my shoulder. "You were dreaming. It was a nightmare, wasn't it? Something you've dreamed many times before. That's why you're barging around."

"I'm not ..."

Her arms wrap around my waist, and she rests her head on my back, silencing me. "It's okay. I'm here."

A sudden rush of terror washes over me.

Those words undo me.

Literally make me want to sink to my knees and cry.

That, or run a million miles, as far away as I can get from her.

I don't know what it is about her that scares me so much.

Maybe it's because she forces me to face myself. Or because she gives me something I've not had in such a long time, it scares the living shit out of me.

Love.

Actual love.

Not just the love of my dick or the love for the way I fuck.

But compassionate love. Someone to talk to. Someone who listens.

And it terrifies me ... because I'm not supposed to have that.

I don't deserve it.

And especially not with her. A student. Someone I'm not supposed to want.

But I want her in more ways than just around my dick.

"Fuck ..." I mutter.

"It's okay if you don't wanna talk. I'm still here for you," she says, hugging me even tighter.

I know she does. That's exactly my problem.

I'm on the verge of giving in, and it's not supposed to happen.

I can't tell her anything ... because it's the greatest shame I have.

And that says a lot, considering I'm fucking one of my students.

I place my hand over my eyes and brush away the impending tears. Sucking in a breath, I say, "Let's go to bed."

"You sure?" she says.

"Yeah, I feel much better now." I turn around and wrap my arms around her. "Thank you."

"You're welcome." She pats my back. "Everyone needs someone sometimes."

I don't.

At least, I didn't use to.

Not until I met her.

Or maybe that was all just a lie in order to stop me from feeling anything when there was no one to turn to.

When we stop hugging, she reaches for my hands and gently pulls me along, back into the bedroom. We crawl back into bed, and right when I lie down, Ninja jumps straight on my balls. I groan and grab them while he lies down next to Hailey, gazing at me with a conceited look.

"Fuck ..." I say.

Hailey laughs. "He hit you right in the nuts, didn't he?"

"Yeah. Fuck you, Ninja." I give him the side-eye. "Just because you're not having pussy doesn't mean you gotta be a dick."

Ninja gets up and starts rubbing his head against my hand.

"Okay ... I forgive you," I say.

"Well, that was quick," Hailey muses.

"How can you not forgive something so adorable." I snuggle him, and Hailey looks at me with a funny face.

"You two make a cute couple together," she jests.

"Shut up," I joke back.

Meanwhile, Ninja jumps back to her side, crawling up next to her.

"It's the first time he's actually come close," Hailey says, holding her hand close so he can smell it.

"Yeah, I think he's less scared of you now that he's seen you a couple of times." Or maybe he's starting to get used to her. Like me.

"Does he always jump on the bed like that?"

"Pretty much. We usually sleep together."

"Hmm … a real bromance then," she muses, making me laugh.

"Hey, nothing against a little kitty love." I pet him a few more times before he curls up into a ball at the end of the bed, near my feet. "You okay with that?" I ask.

"Yeah. He's cute," she says.

"He'll probably steal half your bed in the middle of the night."

"As long as he doesn't kick me out, I'm fine. So long as he doesn't try to do anything funny like scratch my back or lick me. Because this pussy is already taken." She points at herself, laughing, and I laugh too.

I hold her close to my chest, burying my face in her hair. Her scent makes me think of unbridled fun and laughter.

Hailey is here. She's here, and she's not going anywhere.

Just as I need her to be.

For now.

Because it's okay to hold onto someone for a while.

And she's willingly offering a shoulder.

***

Hailey

A few days later

We never really say good-bye.

Not when I leave his home, not when I exit his classroom.

It's as if we both can't get the word to cross our lips.

Even now, when I'm lying in my bed, watching some YouTube on my phone, I still can't get him out of my head. I should be doing homework, but every time I start, my thoughts drift off again. It's useless. I'm way too distracted to even care about college right now.

"Hey, shouldn't you be getting ready for class?" Lesley asks, packing her things.

"Nah, not going."

"Why not?"

"I didn't do the homework, and I'm really not looking forward to getting scolded or getting additional homework."

She makes a face. "Hailey …"

"What? You know it's difficult for me."

"This is your future," Lesley says. "Why else did you go to college?"

"I don't know …" I sigh.

She sucks on her lips. "Lately, I feel like you're not interested anymore. Like you don't even care."

"Well, you're right. Maybe I don't." I sit up straight and prop my pillow under my back. "And yes, I know that's bad, and that I should be trying my best more. I'm just not feeling it right now, okay?"

She frowns. "Why did you apply to college in the first place then?"

I shrug. "To escape, I guess."

"So it's because of your home …"

I nod, rubbing my lips together because I don't really wanna talk about it.

"Well, whatever. I just don't want you to make the wrong decision. I care about you."

I smile at her. "I know you do."

She folds her arms. "And for the love of god, tell me you're not skipping classes because of *him*."

I roll my eyes. "Of course, not." Well, maybe a little, but she doesn't have to know. "He's just a guy."

"Just a guy … or your boyfriend?" she muses, raising a brow at me.

"No … not yet, at least."

She throws her bag over her shoulder. "Well, he sure sounds like a player. Be careful, all right?"

"I will."

"I'm off to psychology. Oh, and I'll be staying at a friend's room for the night. Since you're not taking this class, I figured I needed an extra study buddy. Okay? See ya later."

"Sure. See ya." I wave her off and continue scrolling on my phone.

Suddenly, my phone buzzes in my hand, and I stare at it for a second before I realize I'm being called.

When I notice the name on the screen, my heart stops beating.

Everything turns red in front of my eyes.

For a second, I contemplate ignoring his calls, but I know that won't make him go away. It will only make him try harder, call me longer, maybe even make him come here. Anything but that.

With trembling fingers, I press the call button, and with sweaty palms, I bring the phone to my ear.

"Hailey," I say.

"Goddammit, finally you pick up."

I swallow away the lump in my throat. "What do you want?"

"You. Why haven't you visited? Your mom wants to know why you're ignoring her."

"I'm not ignoring her," I say, sitting up in my bed. "I've replied to all her texts."

"Why wouldn't you come to visit your mom, huh? Do you care that little about her? And what about me? You never call, you never write. It's like you don't even exist."

"Well, sorry," I say, frowning. Really? Is that why he's calling? To make me feel bad?

"I'm done with this. You want to get on my bad side? You'll get my bad side. You're coming home. Right now."

What?

How could he even say that?

Why would he want me to come home? He doesn't miss me.

But my mom does. And now that I'm gone, he can't use me against her anymore.

That's what this is all about. Control.

"No, I'm in the middle of a semester." I almost crush the phone in my hand.

"I don't care! You've wasted enough time there. You're not getting anywhere."

"How do you know that? My grades are fine."

"Sure, they are." His voice is condescending. "Just like everything else about you. No, I think it's enough now. You've spent enough money on this crap. It's time for you to come home and take care of your mom."

"Why would I? She has you!" I yell, boiling inside.

"You're her goddamn daughter! Act like one!" he spits. "God, you're a fucking disgrace. Always whining, always thinking only about yourself. Me. Me. Me. It's always about you, isn't it? You're just like your mother."

That's it.

"Stop talking about my mother!"

"I'll do whatever the fuck I like," he snaps. "You come home right now, or I'll come and get you myself. It's time you started working, so you can earn back all that money we wasted on you all those years."

"I'm not—"

"You're coming home tomorrow! Or I swear I'll fucking come and get you myself! You hear me, you ungrateful shit? Come. Home. Now."

Lowering the phone, I disconnect the call and throw the phone away. I'm shaking, my whole body in shock as the tears run down my face. I hug my legs and hobble around on the bed, my mind running in circles. What do I do? I don't wanna go, but if I don't, I know he'll come for me. He's done it before; acting out and being violent is his thing. It's the only thing he knows. And the sole thing I hate.

Grinding my teeth, I get off the bed and grab my wallet, phone, and keys, slamming the door on my way out.

I'm not staying here for one more second.

His words have poisoned that room.

I can still hear him in my head, shouting at me that I'm a worthless piece of shit.

All I wanna do is get away.

So I run. I run until my lungs hurt; I run until the tears stop streaming; I run until my feet hurt and my body aches. When I get to town, I go into the nearest bar and sit down on a stool, my mind on blank.

It's reckless. Stupid and dangerous to be here alone.

But I don't care anymore.

I just wanna get drunk.

I order an apple martini and show the bartender my fake ID, which apparently still works even though I'm wearing no make-up. Must be the droopy face that makes me look older. I drink my drink without speaking to anyone, listening to the music in the background, trying to forget.

That's all I ever do.

Try to forget.

The alcohol helps.

I guess I'm not so different from Thomas, after all.

Except maybe he's better at this shit than I am because I know for a fact that I'm unable to stop. I don't want to. I don't have the desire. All I want is to drink until I can't remember shit.

So I order another one and chug it down.

That's when a man comes to sit next to me, smiling awkwardly as he orders a beer.

"Hey," he says.

"Hi."

"How you doing?"

"Fine."

I try not to engage, but he keeps talking.

"You look like you're having a shitty time," he says.

"Uh-huh."

"Let me order a drink for you." He beckons the bartender. "Another appletini for the lady over here."

The bartender pours me another one, and I thank him for it, as well as the man beside me, but really, I just want him to shut up.

"So where you from?" he asks.

"Sorry, but I'm here to just be alone for a while. No offense."

"Oh, wow, settle down, girl. No need to get angry."

I side-eye him. "I'm not angry. I just wanna be left alone. Thanks for the drink, though."

"Sure." He makes a face. "Take a drink from a man and then act like that. Classy."

"I never said I was, and I never asked for a drink." I scoot it across the bar to him. "Here, you drink it."

"No thanks," he says, shoving it back so hard, it spills on my shirt.

"Hey! Fuck," I growl, swiping away the alcohol. "Goddammit."

"Sorry. Maybe you should've just been nice," he says, and I give him the stink-eye.

I hop off my stool and go into the bathroom to grab some tissues I can dry my shirt with, but it's not much help. When I try to leave the bathroom, the guy's suddenly in my face.

"Need some help with that?"

"No, I'm good." I try to pass him, but he places his hand on the wall next to me, trapping me inside. "Please …"

"Please what? You know, it wouldn't hurt you to be thankful for a drink."

"A drink that you spilled all over my shirt? Gee, thanks." I raise a brow at him. "Can you please move?"

"No, not until you tell me your name."

"I don't wanna tell you my name. I'm not interested. Do I have to spell it out for you?"

"Oh, c'mon …" He grabs my wrist, which is when I pull back.

"*Don't* touch me."

"What's your problem?" He makes a face. "Stop acting like you're not interested. I know you don't have a boyfriend. Why else would you come to this bar alone?"

"That's none of your fucking business. Now, let me through." Each time I try to pass him, he shoves me back into the bathroom, until the door closes behind us and I'm left alone with a man twice my size.

"Get. Out," I growl.

"Or what?" He laughs, stepping closer.

I quickly rummage through my purse and take out the pepper spray my mom told me to carry. "Or I'll use this."

"Ooh … and I'm supposed to be scared of that?" He shakes his head.

Out of fear that something will happen, I also grab my phone and speed-dial Thomas. It's the first number I pass after …

"Come here." The guy suddenly steps forward and reaches for my hand.

"Get off me!" I yell as we fight over the can of pepper spray.

Meanwhile, I hear Thomas's voice shouting in the back. "Hailey? Hailey?"

"Thomas! Help!" I scream, and in the heat of the moment, I still somehow manage to tell him which bar I'm at. A second later, the guy shoves me so hard I fall to the ground.

"Bitch," he says, spitting on the floor. "You want to use fucking pepper spray on me?"

"Stay away!" I say, crawling backward.

"Fuck that." He throws the can far away in a corner, and his eyes zoom in on me. "I give you a nice cocktail for free, and this is the thanks I get? I should've earned a kiss at least, but with you acting like this … I earn way more than just that."

"No!" I yell, kicking as he comes closer. I try to make him lose his balance, but when he has me by the throat, I'm no match. "C'mon then, a little kiss for the trouble and I might let you go."

When his lips inch closer, I muster all my strength and punch him in the side, causing him to buck and heave.

"Fucking bitch." He coughs, almost choking on his own breath. "You fucking punched me."

I use the last bit of strength to kick him in the head, making him topple over on his back, and then I land another kick right to his balls.

He yowls like a fucking wolf, and I use the time he spends cupping his lady-bits to make a run for the door. Too bad he's grabbed my foot halfway there.

"You're not going anywhere."

"Let me go!" I yell. "You fucking asshole!"

"Asshole? Me? You're the asshole," he growls, trying to pull me back.

I kick him again. "Do you always put your hands on girls without their permission?"

"If they're asking for it, yeah." He tries to crawl on top of me, but I keep kicking him, trying to fend him off. His nose is bleeding because of it, and the blood is pouring onto my pants.

Suddenly, the door opens, and when I look up, I see a face that makes me want to curl up in a ball and cry.

"Thomas!"

Chapter 22

THOMAS

"What the fuck …" I mutter, witnessing the scene in front of me.

I grab Hailey's hand and help her up, holding her close to me as I watch the man on the floor crawl backward.

"I didn't do nothing, man," he says.

"Fuck you!" Hailey spits at him. "Fuck you for trying to put your hands on me."

Rage.

Rabid fury storms through my mind, blocking out all sensible thoughts.

"He … touched you?" I murmur.

"Nuh-uh," the guy says, shaking his head.

"I wasn't talking to you!" I growl, and I grab Hailey's

face with both hands. "What did he do? Did he hurt you?"

"No, he just tried to kiss me, but I didn't let him," she says, and I look her deep in the eye to make sure she isn't lying. "But I hurt him."

I look at the guy and his bleeding nose as he grabs his crotch with a painful look on his face.

"You …"

Like a small boy, he covers his face with his hands and cries. "Please, don't!"

I try to step toward him to show him what it means to feel afraid, but Hailey grabs my hand, stopping me. "Don't," she says with a soft voice, almost as if she regrets saying it already.

"Why?" I glance at her over my shoulder. "Give me one good reason not to smack him straight to hell."

"I just … I just wanna go home. Can we just go home, please?"

Grinding my teeth, I gaze at her and then at that bastard who dared to touch my girl. "You … Apologize to her. Now!"

I make a gesture with my palm, which is enough to make him beg. "I'm sorry, I'm sorry!"

"You won't ever touch another girl without her agreeing, you hear me?" I growl.

"He's been drinking. Actually, we were both drinking …" Hailey muses.

"No excuse for fucked-up behavior," I growl. "Fucking disgrace."

"I'm sorry, okay? I didn't mean to. I just wanted to give her a kiss after offering her a drink, that's all. I was going to let her go. It got out of hand."

"Sure you fucking were," I spit, challenging him by making a fist.

However, Hailey tugging at my coat makes me turn around. "Please? I just wanna go."

I would love nothing more than to beat up that piece of shit who tried to touch my girl, but she keeps insisting, and I can't tell her no. Not when something like this has happened.

I take a deep breath and nod. "Okay."

She rubs her lips together as I place my hand on her shoulder and help her out of the bathroom slowly. One final glance at the man and I know he'll never try that shit again. Just that one look should make him shit his pants.

When it comes to being mad, no one beats me—not with dirty looks and certainly not with fists.

All those months of training in the gym were for this. So I can do justice to those who deserve it.

Hailey shivers in my arms as we walk outside the bar, so I take off my coat and wrap it around her shoulders. "Are you sure you're okay?"

"Yeah," she says, but her voice catches in her throat. "I'm fine."

"Really? Maybe we should call the cops and report it."

"No." She frowns, looking down at the ground. "I don't wanna spend one more second on this. I just wanna forget." She looks up at me with teary eyes that break me in half. "Can I just forget?"

I pull her close and wrap my arms around her, and she lets her head rest against my chest, breathing out a few hiccup-like breaths.

"Let's go home," I murmur, planting a kiss on top of

her hair.

"Thank you for coming," she whispers. "I needed you."

"I know you did," I say, smiling at her, but my smile quickly dissipates. "But I came too late."

"No, it's my fault …" She shakes her head. "I should've never come here. God, I feel so sick." She rubs her stomach as we walk to my car.

"You sure you're going to be okay?"

"I won't barf all over your car, if that's what you're worried about," she says, laughing it off a bit as she sits down in the passenger seat.

"I'm not. I'm worried about you," I say.

She looks at me with a surprised gaze, and I give her a tiny smile before closing the door and going to the driver's side. I hop in and start the engine, trying to let the sound drown out the roar in my heart that tells me to go back into the bar and beat the living shit out of that asshole. But her calm eyes bore into me, and she grasps my hand and holds it tight, keeping me in place. Keeping me in the here and now. It's like she always manages to pull me back from the dark.

"Let's go," I say, clearing my throat, and I turn out of the parking lot and drive off.

I bring her to her place, not mine. I think she needs something familiar now, something where she'll feel at ease. When we're in her room, she sits down on her bed and stares at me with eyes that remind me of death.

I clear my throat again. "Well, I'll be going then."

As I turn around, she says, "Stay. Please."

I sigh, look down at my shoes, and think it over.
Should I?

This is a dorm room, and I'm her teacher.

I shouldn't be anywhere near this place, let alone be alone with her. Yet how could I leave? Not when she begs me like that.

"Are you sure? This is your place. Not mine. I don't … belong here."

"But I do, and you belong with me." Her words strangle me, suffocate me with a kind of love I can't ignore. "Like I belong to you," she continues. "Right?"

I don't respond.

I don't even know how.

"Can you stay? For me?" she asks.

For a moment, I let my head rest against the door.

It's too late to turn the knob and open it.

It's too late to run.

I already made my choice long ago.

With a soft smile on my face, I turn around and walk toward her. I sit down beside her on her bed, which feels like it might collapse under my weight. I bobble around on it, and she looks at me funnily.

"Quite a bed," I say. "You sleep in this?"

"Every day," she says, crawling up her bed further and pulling up her legs so she can hug them.

"Hmm …" I turn my head toward her. "I think it's due for an upgrade."

She laughs. "Really? That's what you're gonna say?"

"Well, I just think you deserve a better night's sleep. That's all."

"Right … well, I don't have the money for that, as much as I'd like to."

"I do."

She frowns, then blushes as I smile at her.

Maybe I can buy her one sometime.

"So ... how are you feeling?" I ask. "Does it hurt anywhere?"

"No, but I do feel like shit," she says. "Mostly because of the alcohol."

"How much did you have to drink?"

"Too much ..." She shakes her head like she can't believe she did that.

"Why?" I ask.

Her face turns sour. "I don't know ..."

"Yes, you do," I muse, looking at her directly. "You just don't want to tell me."

"Maybe," she says after a while.

The silence is deafening, and I put my arm around her shoulder and pull her close. A single tear rolls down her cheek, and I lift my finger to her face to wipe it off. I hate to see her cry. Hate seeing her hurt, no matter in what way, but it chews at my heart.

"You can tell me," I whisper, hugging her close.

"I don't like talking about it," she says, looking frustrated. "Especially not to ..."

"Strangers?"

"But you're not a stranger."

I cup her chin and caress her softly. "I'm no stranger, and I don't want to be. You can tell me anything, Hailey. Even the bad stuff."

She swallows and nods slowly. "It's my mom's boyfriend. He called and told me I need to quit college and come back home."

My eyes widen. "What? Why?"

"Because he's an asshole and wants me to feel

miserable." She frowns. "He treats my mom and me like shit. Always has."

"Fuck … What now?"

"I don't know. Knowing him, he'll come and get me himself. His threats aren't empty; that I do know."

"Jesus …" I sigh and run my fingers through my hair. "Is this what's been bothering you?"

"Not just this. There's always something going on in my 'family.'" She makes quotation marks with her fingers. "If you can call that a family. We haven't been one since my dad …"

She chokes up.

I caress her back softly, trying to encourage her to speak, even though anger rips me apart. I want to know more about her mom's boyfriend so I can pound some common sense into him, but I know I need to be here for her now.

"My dad …" she murmurs. "He died when I was just a kid. Cancer. Fuck. Fucking fuck cancer."

Another tear runs down her cheek. "I still miss him every single day." She rubs her earrings and stares off into space for a while.

"He gave you those ice-cream earrings?" I ask.

She lifts her head with a surprised look on her face. "Who told you that?"

"You did. In the restaurant, remember?"

"Oh … right. Yeah. My dad gave them to me when I was little. I always used to love getting ice cream with him at a shop right at the corner of our street. I loved it so much that he gave me these as a birthday present. It was such a long time ago, and it was before …"

"Before your mom's new boyfriend."

She takes a deep breath and lets it out again. "He ruined our life. Mom only liked him because he was arrogant. He swept her off her feet and took her to places, gave her lots of gifts, and showered her with love. It was her way of forgetting about my dad. Not much left of that sweetness now."

"I don't think she'll forget about your dad," I say.

"Oh no, but she tries. That's why she wants to stay with him so badly."

"Your mom's boyfriend?"

"Yeah. She craves his attention, even when it's bad. Wants to do right in his eyes, but nothing is ever right for him."

"Did he hurt you?" I ask after a while.

She licks her lips. "Sometimes. But mostly my mom. They're always fighting and yelling. I don't remember anything else about my childhood after my dad died other than him hitting my mother and my mother not even defending herself."

"Jesus …" I take another deep breath. I can't believe what I'm hearing.

She suddenly grabs my arm. "Please, don't tell anyone," she says.

What am I supposed to say?

All I can think of is calling the cops and telling them all about the abuse she and her mother have endured. Then again, what evidence do I have other than her story? Nothing. It's useless. I feel so goddamn useless.

But her voice pulls me from my thoughts and back into the moment. "Please?"

I nod and grab her so I can hug her tight. "I promise."

God, no wonder she's so closed-off. She's already been through so much.

In my arms, she finally relaxes, and the tears start flowing again.

Fuck. It really hurt her bad.

Not only did her mom's boyfriend fuck it up for her, but then she went to drink her fears away, only to be attacked in the bathroom.

Fuck me.

I should've been there for her.

Should've been with her when it happened.

"I'm sorry. I didn't mean to start bawling all over you," she says, sniffing.

"It's okay." I smile, looking down at her, and I brush through her hair. "Cry if you need to. I'm here."

"Please don't leave …" she mutters.

I press a kiss on top of her head. "I won't. I promise."

She nods and buries her head in my shirt again.

Always so strong yet so fragile. And all I want to do is hold her and tell her it'll be okay. I want to take away her pain, but I know I can't. Her cries penetrate my bones, and they make me never want to let go.

I recognize that type of cry. A cry that only comes out once in a million years. A cry holed up for so long, she probably didn't even know it had to come out.

I understand.

I won't run.

I won't hide from her pain.

I'll console her as long as she needs me.

Because it's the only thing I can do right.

Chapter 23

THOMAS

I wake up covered in sweat and with the realization that I'm not in my own fucking bed.

Fuck.

Fuck, fuck, fuck!

I throw the blanket off me and jump out of her bed, looking around for my stuff.

Apparently, things got so complicated yesterday, with her needing my support, that I didn't want to leave. We talked all night until we eventually dozed off together.

And now, it's fucking morning.

Normally, there wouldn't be any problem with this fact, other than that I'm in a student's dorm room.

If I get caught, my career is ruined.

Fuck.

I search for my clothes and put them on quickly, dancing around on one foot as I slip on my pants and frantically throw things in search of my phone.

"What are you doing?" Hailey mumbles, scratching her hair. Her face is still red from yesterday's tears.

"Getting out of here," I say as I tuck my keys into my pocket and put on my coat.

"Why?" She yawns and stretches her arms.

"I can't be seen here," I say.

Her eyes suddenly burst open. "What?"

"It's not you. It's because I'm your teacher, remember?" I give her a quick kiss on the cheek. "I gotta run. See you in class, okay?"

"Okay," she says, turning her head to sneak a quick kiss on the lips. She grins. "I can't wait."

"Act as normal as you can," I say, "and don't make a scene."

"Right." She nods as I leave her room, and she yells something at me. "Thank you for staying with me!"

"Don't mention it!" I call back and quickly run down the stairs and out of the building.

I hurry to the parking lot and unlock the car, jumping in fast before anyone can see me. Hopefully, all of this will go unnoticed. We haven't been caught so far, but we really need to be careful. At least, if we're going to keep this up.

As I drive off, I can't help but wonder if we really are going to keep doing this.

If we'll drift in this limbo forever.

If it's ever going to be more than just sex.

If it ever was just that.

***

Hailey

When I get to school, I no longer feel the heavy burden of having to deal with my mom's boyfriend. After that cry-party last night, I feel much stronger, and I know I won't let him stomp all over me again. He can come get me himself if he wants, but I'll greet him with a fucking shovel.

In class, I can't keep my eyes off Thomas. He's always so cocky, and he always exudes an aura that makes people look at him. He radiates power—but not the bad kind, the noble kind. When I said I was falling head over heels for him, that was an understatement.

His class is pretty much the only one I pay attention in, mostly because of his face and that smile.

After class, I wait until everyone is gone and then follow him to his office. He picks up a stack of papers as I close the door, the noise making him look over his shoulder.

"Hailey."

I jump in his arms and smash my lips onto his, surprising him.

When our lips unlatch, he smiles and shakes his head. "Okay, what did I do?"

"Nothing," I muse. "I just wanted to do that."

"Hmm . . . do it again." He licks his lips, and I lean forward for another peck.

"Are you feeling better?" he asks.

"Yeah, much better. I had a bit of a headache earlier

because of the apple martinis I had, but I took a painkiller, and it's gone now."

"Good ..." He grabs a sheet of paper and holds it out to me. "Now that you're here, I wanted to give you this. It's a test so you can see if you'll pass the actual test."

"So it's a cheat sheet?" I say, frowning.

"No, these are different questions," he says, smiling. "Hey, I would *never* abuse my power."

I narrow my eyes at his witty comment. "Right ..."

Suddenly, the door slams open. I turn my head in shock, dropping almost everything in my hands.

"Natalie?" Thomas's voice sounds much higher than normal.

Natalie.

That woman ... She's the one I saw him with when she drove him to school that one time. The one Lesley was talking about. Oh, god.

"Come with me," she says, holding open the door like some bulldog with a face that matches.

Thomas doesn't even protest. He just takes a deep breath and walks right past me.

"Thom—Sir?" I say, quickly catching myself in the act of being unprofessional.

"He won't be here for a while, so it's better if you just go home," Natalie says, and she places her hand on Thomas's back as she escorts him out.

A chill runs up and down my spine seeing her walk with him.

I go out after them, but when Thomas glances at me over his shoulder with a look that predicts thunder, I know I can't go with him.

***

THOMAS

I stand in the middle of the room as she slams the door shut and sits her ass down on top of the desk in the corner. I cross my arms when she gazes at me with a criticizing look.

"I told you to quit doing what you were doing," she says. "It's not just rumors anymore now. I just heard from a student that he saw you in a girl's dorm room."

My stomach turns upside down, and I suck in a breath to keep myself together.

"Is it true? You're sleeping with a student?" She makes it sound like it's disgusting.

I nod, frowning.

"Jesus, Thomas …" She sighs and rubs her forehead with her palm. "Goddammit. Why'd you have to do this?"

There's no point in denying it now. "It just happened, okay? We met in a club. I didn't know she was a student."

"Yeah, well, you blew it. You should've quit it as soon as you found out, and now, I discover you've been fooling around with her behind my back?"

"It's not like that."

"Yes, it is," she snaps. "It's time you stopped denying it and faced what you did. After everything I did for you … this is how you repay me?"

"This has nothing to do with you." My hand balls into a fist.

"Yes, it does because now I'm faced with a dilemma I

don't know how to solve. Don't you realize you've gone too far? You can't fix this anymore, Thomas. It's too late."

Fuck. I swallow away the lump in my throat. Is she doing what I think she's doing?

"Sit down," she says.

"No ..." I shake my head. I can't believe it.

After all the trouble I went through to hide my affair with Hailey, it still got out.

"You know there's no other option."

"Fuck that," I say, refusing to acknowledge what's happening. "I'm outta here," I say, turning around.

"Wait! We're not done talking yet."

"I am," I growl.

I storm out the door before she has a chance to say another word.

I don't want to hear it.

I don't want to know.

I don't want to realize that I fucked up ... and that there's no going back from here.

***

Hailey

As I walk through the school building, more people are looking at me than usual. I mean, I get that a red bob draws attention, but I've never had this many eyeballs on me. Could it be the earrings? Just in case, I take them off and tuck them in my pocket. Still, people are looking at me, and not just that ... they're whispering too. And laughing.

Someone bumps into me and giggles when she sees me, exchanging looks with her friends.

One of them whispers into her ear, and I can just catch a few words.

"She's *that* girl."

That girl?

I walk past them only for more stares to find me in the cafeteria.

It's as if everyone suddenly knows who I am.

Or worse.

They know something I don't.

I hurry to the vending machine and get a Snickers before running off again.

While I walk, I still hear them talk behind my back.

"Look, it's her."

"Who?"

"That girl they're talking about."

Who is they? Is it everyone? Why? What do they know?

Panic zaps through me as I walk fast, trying to get away from the people who seemingly know me for no other reason other than rumors. I don't even know what's going on or how they all suddenly found out.

I go into the bathroom to try to escape it all. That's when I run into Lesley.

"Hailey, oh my god, have you heard the rumors that are being spread around?" She grabs my arm and pulls me aside.

"Yes, but I don't get it. What are they saying?" I ask

She looks around to see if anyone's snooping before leaning in and whispering, "Everyone knows about your fling with Mr. Hard."

"What?"

My throat clamps up, and I struggle to breathe.

"Listen, someone found out. They saw him leaving our dorm room, and then rumors started spreading. It's been going on since this morning, but most of it is about Mr. Hard."

My heart beats in my throat.

"They all know it's me …" I mutter.

"Some girl found out who was living in our dorm room, and at first, they thought it was me, but then one of them remembered they'd seen you two together an awful lot lately. They put two and two together … and well, the whole school is talking about it."

"The whole school is talking about it?" I repeat.

"I'm sorry, Hailey."

"Everyone knows I'm screwing my professor?" I say, tears welling up in my eyes.

"I'm really sorry." Lesley pulls me in for a hug. "God, I wish it never happened. But you should've been more careful. Why did you invite him to our home?"

"I don't know … so many things happened. My mom's boyfriend called. I needed him," I say, still not getting to terms with the fact that everyone knows.

But then it hits me.

If they know about me … they know about him, as well. Thomas.

"Oh, god." I slap my hand in front of my mouth.

"What?" Lesley asks as I pull myself out of her embrace.

"He's gonna lose his job," I mutter. "Shit. Shit!"

"Calm down. What do you mean lose his job?"

"He's a professor. I'm his student. Everyone knows," I

say, pacing around in the bathroom.

"Oh ... damn. I hadn't thought about that. His reputation will be ruined."

"Exactly." I run my fingers through my hair. "And it's all my fault."

She cocks her head and sighs. "Don't say that."

"It is. I practically seduced him to continue with our affair. He wanted to quit, but I wouldn't let him."

"He agreed on his own. He's a grown man. He's responsible for his own mistakes," she says, but I'm not listening anymore.

I feel so guilty.

So bad.

I just have to go to him.

"I'm gonna see if he's in his office."

"He's not. I already checked." She clears her throat when I look confused. "When I heard the rumors, I wanted to go tell him, but he wasn't there. Do you think he's gone home? Maybe he knows too."

I take a deep breath and sigh. "I don't know, but I'm going after him."

"What? Wait," she says as I open the door. "And then what? What are you gonna do when you get there?"

I shrug. "I don't know, but anything's better than staying here where everyone's talking about me. I'm now *that* girl."

"That'll blow over. You know they don't remember this shit," she says as I walk out.

I glance at her over my shoulder. "Still, I fucked up. I *have* to go talk with him."

"All right ... well, just take care of yourself, okay? I'll be in our dorm room if you need me," she says.

"Thanks," I say, smiling at her, but it's all fake. On the inside, I'm burning. Burning with rage. Burning with regret.

If only I'd been more careful.

Then it wouldn't all have gone to shit.

***

Thirty minutes later

As I run up to his apartment, I hear voices yelling from afar. For a second, I contemplate leaving again, but my curiosity is too strong to deny. I wanna know what's going on, so I sneak up to the door and listen in on a conversation I know I shouldn't be hearing.

"Please, just leave me alone," Thomas says with a low, defeated voice.

"No. I followed you here for a reason. You might think you've gotten off easily by storming off like that, but I don't accept it." It's the woman's voice.

"I never said I had it easy or that I want it to be easy! I just want it to be over." His voice fluctuates in tone.

"Tough shit, Thomas. You should've told me what was going on. Should've been honest with me." It sounds like her, the woman that came to his office. Natalie.

"It's none of your business," he growls.

"Yes, it is! And you know damn well why!" She sighs out loud. "You've been acting so strange lately, and now, I know why. I told you to get your shit together, to stop drinking and finally pick up your life, and what do you do?

You fuck it up with one of your own fucking students."

"I know!" I hear glass shattering, and it makes me jolt against the wall. I almost lose my balance, but I catch myself on the doorpost. "Dammit, don't tell me what I already know."

"Then you also know you have no right to be pissed off at your own mistake. I'm the one who should be pissed off. You slept with a student. How am I supposed to think that's right?"

"You don't," he says.

"Of course, not! Goddammit ... After everything I did for you."

Everything she did for him?

"This is how you repay me?" she adds.

"Please ... just leave me alone," he mutters.

"No. I *need* an explanation."

"I don't have one, okay?" he yells. "It just happened. We fucked. A few times. It didn't mean anything."

Didn't mean anything?

Tears well up in my eyes again, but I blink them away.

My heart is breaking slowly.

And when I thought it couldn't break anymore, she opens her mouth again.

"It's done. You're done. I'm done. Over. I quit."

She quits.

They're done.

With trembling hands, I release the doorpost, only to stagger forward.

I thought it couldn't be true, but apparently, it is.

Without thinking, I peek through the open door and look at the both of them, stampeding through his room.

He's rubbing his face while hers reminds me of thunder and lightning.

I suppose it's only fitting ... for an angry girlfriend.

Because that's what it's always been.

Right?

That's what I was afraid to see. Afraid to admit.

That moment when she dropped him off, I should've believed Lesley. Shouldn't have ignored that looming feeling of betrayal.

Because damn ... what a sad thing to find out that you're not the only one.

That it's all just been a fling.

And I fell for it.

All along, I could've known. I could've asked, but I didn't.

I let us stay in limbo. And now, I pay the price.

With tear-stained eyes, I stand in front of his door, not giving a shit if either of them sees me.

When they look up and see me, their faces turn cold with sweat, and his eyes grow big.

I stand strong, even though I feel weak and broken.

But I refuse to let him see.

I refuse to be his victim.

I will stand as he falls.

And when his lips part, I turn away and run.

Run as fast as I can, away from his apartment, for the last time.

Chapter 24

THOMAS

Fuck.

Fuck, fuck, fuck!

"Hailey!" I yell, but she's already disappeared from view the moment I step out my door.

"Let her go," Natalie says, and she places her hand on my shoulder. "It's not worth it."

"Dammit, she heard everything," I say, shaking her hand off. "I knew it. I knew I never should've let you in. Look what happened."

"That's all on you," she says. "You should've dealt with it when you had the chance."

"It? Her name is Hailey."

"And now her name is 'gone-girl,'" she jests. "It's too

late, Thomas. She won't come back, trust me."

I look out the window, but I can't see her anywhere, not even in the parking lot. Fury makes me slam my fist into the wall. "Fuck!"

"Calm down," she says. "It's not gonna help you."

"I have to go after her," I say.

"No, don't. You've already ruined your career. Don't ruin her too."

"But she hates me," I growl.

"Then it's only easier for her to let you go. It wouldn't have worked out anyway." She rubs my back. "I mean, look at you two. She's young; you're not. You have a job; she doesn't. You already have a whole history behind you. She's only just starting out. She's different than you are. Your lives don't match. It could never have been more than a fling."

I hear her words, but they don't register because I don't want them to.

Part of me wants to cling to the hope that I can salvage something. And a part of me just wants to give up the fight.

"Let her go. If she hates you, then that means at least you won't have to break her heart when she loves you," she says. "It's easier to hate than to love."

"And now, we're both broken beyond repair," I mutter, resting my head against the window.

"Maybe you should've thought about that before you played with her heart," she says, turning away. "You gambled, and you lost. It's time to admit your defeat and rescue whatever you can."

"I can't. I'm already fired."

"Hmm … true." She takes a deep breath as she walks to the door. "But at least you can now focus on something worthwhile instead of a young girl who would never be happy with you anyway."

As she walks out the door, I glance over my shoulder and say, "You're wrong. You're wrong about her. And about me."

She pauses but doesn't reply. Then she closes the door behind her and leaves behind a gaping emptiness that makes me howl with pain.

***

Hailey

A few days later

I totally screwed up the test I had today.

I knew I was going to fail it the moment I sat down to pen my answers.

I hadn't studied.

I hadn't even tried.

Well, I did, but I couldn't get past the first page without sobbing uncontrollably.

I can't do anything for shit, and I hate it.

I hate feeling weak. I hate feeling betrayed.

But most of all, I hate Thomas Hard.

He ripped my heart out of my chest and stomped on it in front of the entire school.

I'll never forgive him.

At least, that's what I tell myself. That I can hate him forever, even though I know I can't.

All I want is for this deceit to go away. For it to have

never existed in the first place.

Is it so wrong for a girl to want a happy life with the guy she fell in love with?

Love ... what a waste that I gave it away.

Just like that.

In my room, I sit and stare out the window, listening to music on my headphones while trying not to think about Thomas, which is obviously not working. I'm trying to decide whether it's even worth it to go on with my semester. I'm failing all my classes, and the whole school recognizes me as 'that girl' or worse ... some even whisper 'whore' behind my back.

It hurts, but not as much as him not being here to apologize does.

I haven't seen him since I last saw him in his apartment with Natalie.

His office is empty, completely stripped of anything that would remind me of him. It's as if he's completely vanished off the face of the earth. And I'm still here ... alone, miserable.

I sigh, pick up my pillow, and shove it in my own face, growling.

"C'mon, Hailey. Move the fuck on. He's not worth it."

If only Lesley were here so we could binge watch *Sex and The City*, but unlike me, she actually goes to her classes. Like right now.

Out of nowhere, my phone starts buzzing, and I jump out of bed to fish it off the table. My excitement quickly dies out when I notice the number isn't one I recognize.

"Hello?" I say as I pick up.

"Hi, is this Hailey Walters?"

"Yeah, that's me." I don't recognize the voice.

"All right. This is Saint Lucas's Hospital. Your mother's been admitted."

My heart stops beating. "What's going on? What happened?"

"She's had significant bruising and a fractured rib. We don't know the cause yet, but it's imperative that you come here as soon as possible. She gave your number as a contact."

"Oh, my god. Yes, I'm on my way right now!" I grab my stuff as quickly as possible and run out the door, not giving a shit about the fact that I have classes in a few hours. My mom comes first.

***

When I get to the hospital, I immediately ask for her room number and make my way upstairs. My heart is racing, and sweat is running down my back as I hurry through the hallways to my mom's room. When I finally find her, she's lying in bed with her eyes closed, and I fear the worst.

"Mom!" With tears in my eyes, I run to her bedside and hug her tight, but she's not responding.

"Hi, I see you've arrived." A nurse comes in.

"Hi," I say, rubbing my hair out of my wet face. "Why isn't she awake?"

"She's still asleep from the anesthetics. She's been given a lot of morphine to deal with the pain.

"Oh ... What happened?" I ask as I sit down on the chair beside her.

The nurse hangs a new bag of antibiotics on her line and

checks my mom's stats. "Well, we don't really know exactly, as she seemed to have been quite confused about it. She uttered some words to the paramedics about stairs. We think she may have fallen down. It's amazing she even managed to call us."

I look at the bruises on her face and say, "I don't think those were caused by falling down the stairs."

She raises her brows. "It's possible. We don't know. She didn't say much other than to call you."

"Okay." I purse my lips. "What about my mom's boyfriend?"

"Ahhh ... Yes, we called him too. He hasn't said a lot other than to say she fell down the stairs."

"Right." I frown.

"I think he's getting some coffee. If you want some too, you can get it down the hall on the left." She smiles.

"No thanks," I say. "I just wanna stay with my mom for a second. If that's okay."

"Of course. I'll leave you two to it. Oh, she might wake up soon. The morphine dosage has been reduced, so she won't feel so drowsy all the time."

"Thank you," I say as she leaves the room.

I take a deep breath and then caress my mom's cheek. "Oh, Mom ... what did he do to you?"

Her mouth twitches and a soft moan leaves her throat. I smile, blinking away the tears. "Shh... don't talk yet."

"Oh, so you're here too. Couldn't get here sooner?"

The moment I hear his ugly voice, I turn around and growl, "This is all your fault."

"What? You not being here?" He snorts. "That's all on you, girl."

"Don't talk to me. You've said enough," I say. "I don't want you anywhere near my mom or me."

"Well, tough luck, kid, because this is my woman."

"She is *not* yours. She's not an object you own. She's a human being, and I know she didn't just *fall* down the stairs either."

He makes a face. "What? You're not suggesting I did it? Bullshit."

My mom suddenly squints her eyes, and I immediately focus on her again. "Mom!" I grab her hand and squeeze. "I'm here."

"Hailey?" Her hand lifts and she wipes her forehead. "God, I'm glad you're here." She's still slurring, but I can understand her just fine.

"And I'm not going anywhere either," I say, squeezing her hand tighter.

"I had such a bad dream. And I feel so sleepy. Like I've been asleep for days."

"That's the drugs," I say, chuckling a little.

"Yeah, and because she's a lazy twat."

"Shut up!" I say, turning around. "Just shut up."

Infuriated, he slams his coffee cup down on the table and says, "How dare you speak to me like that?"

"Stop ..." my mom mutters.

"No, you need to learn how to behave."

"And you need to learn to keep your hands off my mom," I growl.

"What did you say?" His brows are on six o'clock, and his fists are balled.

"You heard me; I know this was your doing."

"If she weren't such a clumsy woman, she wouldn't trip

down the stairs all the time. Don't you blame this on me, kid; you weren't even there for her. You were too busy screwing other boys at that stupid college of yours where you're not learning one damn thing."

"Please ... don't fight ..." my mom utters.

Tears well in my eyes. "You know nothing about me. Or my mom. I don't give a damn what you say—I know you hit her. Those bruises on her face didn't happen because she 'fell down the stairs.'" I make quotation marks with my fingers.

"Hailey ..." my mom says.

"No, Mom, I'm done faking it. I'm done lying. You should be too. Look at what he did to you."

I direct my attention back to him. "You're the only reason our whole world went to shit. You ruined everything. Me. My mom. You're a bastard."

"That's it!"

He lifts his fist and makes a threatening move.

Right then, a nurse enters the room, and he quickly lowers his arm and pretends he was stretching and yawning. Then he leaves the room again, eyeballing the nurse with some kind of non-verbal threat. The nurse just stands there and furrows her brows at him, turning her head to look at him as he stomps off.

"Quite a piece of work," she says. "Excuse me."

"I know, right?" I say.

"Hailey ..." My mom coughs.

"I *hate* him." I grab her hand and look her deep in the eyes. "Mom, please ..."

"I'm sorry, Hailey," she says, her eyes turning watery.

I rub my lips together, trying to prevent the tears on my

side. "I know."

"No, you don't. I'm really sorry I put you in this position again."

"I'm okay, Mom, really. I am. Worry about yourself."

She leans in to brush her thumb across my cheeks. "Such a beautiful, smart girl. You've got your father's genes, not mine."

I smile. "And your caring and forgiving nature," I say.

"Hailey ..." She pauses. "I lied."

I close my eyes and squeeze her hand again. "I know, Mom. It's okay."

I know exactly what she lied about.

Not just these bruises, but all her other bruises and broken bones too.

All of it.

It was all a lie.

She starts to cry. "I'm sorry ... When he pushed me, he left me there. He just left me for dead. I managed to crawl to the phone and call for help."

"You're lucky he left. He could've done more damage," I say.

She sniffs. "But now, he's gone ... and I don't think he's coming back."

"Good," I say. She rests her head on my shoulder, and I kiss her on the back of the head. "Promise me you'll tell him you two are over for good. End it. Once you're out of the hospital."

She nods softly. "I know you must hate me."

"I don't. I'll never hate you." I give her another peck. "I hate him."

"After your dad died, I needed someone so badly." Her

breathing staggers.

"Don't talk about the past," I say. "Just tell me you'll never let him touch you again. No more bruises. No more broken bones. No more lies."

She nods as the tears roll down her cheeks, and I can't help but cry a little myself too.

Who in the world could make it through without crying when seeing their own mother in shambles?

I know I can't.

"I love you, Mom," I say. "I know you need love, but isn't my love enough?"

"It is." She hugs me even tighter. "It is, Hailey."

Chapter 25

THOMAS

When I've finally mustered up the courage to speak to her, I go to her dorm.

Only to find out she isn't even there.

I've knocked like fifteen times and gotten no response.

It's making me so anxious; I want to smash the fucking door in, but that wouldn't be appropriate. I've even asked if Lesley was there, but she isn't answering either. The only option I have left is calling her cell.

It takes me about fifteen minutes of staring at the screen before I finally press that button.

I know she probably won't want to hear from me and will most likely hang up the phone the moment I say a few words. Understandable. She's completely right too, considering what she heard.

But I don't want to let her go with half of the truth.

I know I should, but I can't.

I just can't get it over my heart to smash hers like that. Even if it's the right decision, like Natalie said.

When I do finally press that call button, the seconds that pass feel like hours, but nothing happens, and I can feel my courage drift.

"Fuck ..." I whisper when I realize it's no use.

Where could she be?

I decide to take a different route. I look through her Facebook posts until I find Lesley, and I click her profile to check for a phone number. Luckily, she let it be visible to friends of friends, so I quickly copy it and call the number.

"Hello?"

"Hi, this is Thomas. Sorry to call, but could you tell me where Hailey is?"

"Oh ... it's you ..."

"Look, I know you must be angry with me, and for the right reasons, but please let me talk to Hailey. If you know where she is, please tell me."

"Why?" she growls.

"Because I want to make things right."

"You already blew that chance, don't you see? You used her ..." she says. "You should've stayed away when you had the chance."

"I know, and I'm sorry, really, I am. I never wanted to break her heart. I ... I ..." I don't want to say these words over the phone, and I don't want to say them to her.

I want to say them to Hailey.

I want to say them when I can see her. Face to face.

"What are you gonna do then, huh? What's left to say?"

"Anything. But I have to explain it to her. Please … she would want me to. You know that."

She grumbles but doesn't go against me. "Fine. If you have to know, she's at Saint Lucas's Hospital."

My jaw drops. "What? Has something happened to her?"

"Not her, her mom."

Oh, god.

This couldn't have come at a worse possible time.

"I'm not there yet, but I will be once I've finished my test. You'd better get there before I do because I can't allow you to hurt her anymore."

"I understand," I say. "Thank you."

She hangs up, and I tuck my phone into my pocket and rush downstairs, back into my car, and race off.

***

30 minutes later

When I finally get there, I immediately go to the service desk and ask for the correct room number. I thank the nurse and rush upstairs and through the corridors until I finally reach the room. As I enter, everything grows quiet, and the moment she sees me, her face turns white.

"Hi," I say, tentatively stepping inside.

"Hello. Who are you?" her mom asks.

She looks drowsy, weak, and definitely bruised. I wonder what happened. She looks like she had quite a rough time.

"I'm Thomas Hard. I'm your daughter's teacher." I frown. "Or at least, I was."

"What are you doing here?" Hailey asks, the look on her face murderous.

"Um ... I just came because ... Well, I don't really know why. I just want to be here for you." I clear my throat when neither of them responds. "Are you okay, ma'am?"

"Well, as fine as can be when you're in the hospital," she muses, chuckling a bit, immediately coughing after.

"What happened?" I ask.

Her mom opens her mouth. "Oh, I fell—"

Hailey throws her mother a look. "Her boyfriend did this."

My jaw drops. "What? Where is he now?" I growl.

Fuck. I never thought it'd go this far, but it does make sense considering what she told me.

"He's gone," her mom says. "He hasn't come back since he tried to hit ... Hailey." She looks down at her blanket. "I think he's trying to get away now that a nurse saw him do it."

"So he's on the run. Dammit ..." I almost want to go after him, but I need to take care of my business here first. "Is there anything I can do for you ladies now that I'm here?" I ask.

"We don't need you here." Hailey's sharp voice cuts through anything.

"I just want to help," I say, smiling, but she won't return my smile.

"And I don't want your help," she snaps.

I frown and rub my lips together looking at the floor. "Please ..."

"Oh, Hailey, c'mon, he's such a nice gentleman," her mom says.

"Mom, no. You don't know him."

"You're right. I don't deserve to be here, and I don't deserve you. I just wanted to talk, that's all. Maybe there's something I can do to make it easier."

"Yeah, you can … by leaving." Her words cut straight into my soul.

Fuck, I really hurt her badly.

"Hailey …" I sigh. "I'm sorry."

"No," she interjects. "Don't. Not here."

I nod slowly, grinding my teeth. "Please, let me explain—"

"Get out," she hisses, getting up from her seat. "Just get out."

I lift my hands. "Okay … okay …"

"Get out!" she yells.

"So you won't give me a chance to explain?" I stare at her for a few seconds, but her lips are sealed shut.

I take a deep breath and nod.

I blew it.

I completely blew it.

Without even getting a chance to fix what I'd broken, I blew it all.

With slumped shoulders, I turn around and leave the room, but the struggle inside isn't over yet. Not by a long shot. Even though I was defeated, I won't give up.

I *need* to make things right.

So the minute I get outside, I take out my phone and start searching through her photos on Facebook until I find a picture of her mom and a tag. I click on her mom's profile and scroll down her timeline until I find what I'm looking for. A picture of the boyfriend. His hand is on her neck, like she's more of a dog than a human being, and behind them is a blue car with a scratched license plate, but I can still make out the numbers.

Gotcha.

Irrational thoughts float through my head as I make my way to the parking lot and search each and every car for the matching numbers. I don't give a damn that it looks suspicious and that people might think I'm nuts. They can stare all they want; I'm not stopping until I find the son of a bitch who dared to hurt the mother of the girl I love.

Yes. Love. Because that's what it fucking is, even if I'm afraid to tell her.

Damn, I'm even afraid to admit it to myself, but I'll be damned if I let this slip. I didn't know it until it was too late, but I love her, and I'm not going to let her go.

Just like I'm not going to let that motherfucker get away.

I don't care if it takes me hours or days to find him, but I *will* find him.

After strolling around the parking lot for a good half hour, I finally come across a license plate that matches the exact numbers on the picture. I grin as I have a closer look and inspect his car, peering through the window. No one is inside, but I see some trash—particularly, a few bags and papers from a fast food restaurant and some french fries on the passenger seat.

Right as I turn around, a man's right up in my face.

"What the fuck are you doing near my car?"

It's him. I recognize him from the pictures. "Well, hello …"

"Do I know you?"

"Yes. Wait. No, we haven't actually met, but ..."

"But what? What are you doing here?" he growls, a despicable look on his face.

"Looking for you." I grin as I look around and notice a few bystanders watching us. "You should've run when you had the chance."

"What?" He makes a face, confused. "Get outta my fucking face."

"Well," I say, smiling like an idiot. "I would, but your fat ass is in the way."

His eyes narrow. "What did you say?"

"Oh, I think you heard me right ..."

"You wanna start a fight?"

"Oh no, I just want to laugh at your poor intellect," I muse, chuckling a little.

"Say it again. I dare you." He balls his fist.

"What? The part where you're fat or stupid?"

A fist suddenly lands on my face.

I stagger, grabbing my face as I hold onto the car for support.

He actually fucking hit me.

Great. Exactly as planned.

"Hmrr ..." I groan, getting back up again.

"There's more where that came from, so unless you want to brawl, I'd suggest you get your ugly ass outta here."

I shrug and rub my jawline. "Yeah, well, see, I'd love to but ... I have something to do."

"What?"

"Well, I have this thing for a girl. You wouldn't believe it if I told you, but just know that I'm not doing this because

I'm an asshole. Well, okay, I am an asshole, but that's beside the point."

"What the fuck are you talking about?" he says, squinting.

"The point is … I don't like fighting, but since you hit me first, that gives me the freedom to defend myself. So thanks …"

I immediately follow up that statement with a punch to his gut.

I don't know why he didn't see it coming because I saw his punch coming from a mile away. I wanted him to hit me, so I let him. It gave me an excuse to pound him.

Another punch to the face and a kick in the gut has him lying on the asphalt, blood dripping from his nose.

"What the fuck, man?" he yells.

"That's for hitting a woman," I spit, and then I kick him in the balls. "And that's for hurting my girl."

"Your girl?"

I lean over him and grab him by the collar, "Hailey," I growl. "Remember that girl you punished for just being alive? Yeah, I know how you treated her like shit. It's going to end today. Because you know what's going to happen? You're going to disappear from their lives forever. You're never going to speak to them, and you're not ever going to try to come close to them again. You hear me?"

He nods profusely as I threaten him with another fist. "I promise."

"Really?" I raise a brow.

He growls and his eyes narrow again. "Fuck, no."

And then we start rolling over the ground, fists flying everywhere.

Chapter 26

Hailey

A few hours later

"All set!" the nurse says as I help my mom out of bed.

"Thank you," I say. "I'm so glad I can take her home in one piece."

"No problem. Make sure to be more careful next time." The nurse smiles and winks as she leaves us alone.

Lesley's here too now to support my mom and me as I help her get to the door. Her broken rib must hurt a lot, but the medicine should dampen it a bit. Lesley grabs my mom's purse, while the nurse and I help my mom into a wheelchair.

"Tell me if you need me to help," Lesley says.

"I'm good," I say, as I glance at her over my shoulder. "But thank you for helping. I really couldn't have gotten through this without you."

"You two seem like very good friends," my mom says. "I'm really glad you're taking such good care of my daughter while you're both in college."

"Of course," Lesley says. "That's what friends are for."

As the nurse pushes my mom to the door, someone knocks and enters. It's a police officer. "Hi, hope I'm not disturbing. I'm detective Fargo. I just wanted to ask some questions if that's okay."

"Um … sure?" I say, looking at my mom. She nods. "All right. Where?"

"Come with me, please." We walk after him into a small office down the hall. The nurse puts my mom's wheelchair next to me as I sit down, while Lesley fetches a glass of water.

"Well, I'll be right back then," the nurse says, scurrying off.

The police officer sits down and pulls out a notepad and a pencil. "So you're in the hospital. How did you end up here?"

My mom looks at me, and I nod at her before she turns her head back to him. "I … was pushed down the stairs."

"By her boyfriend," I interject because she's starting to shake.

Lesley suddenly comes back, and when she notices the tension in the room, she quickly places the glass of water on the table and says, "I'll wait down the hall."

I nod and mouth a thank you to her.

"Does this happen often?"

"Yes, he's done it many times before," I reply. "Mostly just attacking us out of the blue."

"How often did he hit you? Did he hit both of you?" the officer asks when Lesley's gone.

"Yes. He hit my mom more than once, on several occasions. I usually managed to get away in time ... but not always."

"Okay ..." He pens all of it down.

"Why are you asking this?" my mom asks.

"Well, we have your boyfriend in a cell at the station."

My jaw drops. "What? How?"

The officer purses his lips. "I can't go into too much detail, but he was found fighting outside in the parking lot, so we took him in for questioning. He kept asking for you." He points at my mom. "Told us you were here, but when we called, the nurse also told us he'd been violent toward you, so that was a red flag for us."

"Oh, god ..." I mutter.

Finally, it's really happening.

"So I just came here to make sure that my info was correct."

"So you have him in custody?" my mom asks.

"Yes, ma'am." The officer nods and gives her a warm smile. "If you're telling the truth, it means he can be charged in court."

My mom grabs her chest. "Oh, god ..."

"You okay, Mom?" I place a hand on her shoulder.

Tears well up in her eyes. "Yes, I just ... I don't know. It just feels so strange. Like it's going so fast."

"But it's good," I say, reassuring her. "He's supposed to be locked up after what he's done to you all these years."

"I have one final question," the officer asks. "And that's if you'd please come with me to the station."

"Why?" I ask.

"Well, since he's not officially registered as your mother's partner, we need to make sure we have the right guy. And you can make a statement while you're there so we can start the investigation."

"Mom? What do you think?" I ask.

She grabs my hand and squeezes tight. "You're right. It's time to come face to face with my demons." She turns her head toward detective Fargo. "Yes."

"All right." He tucks his note and pencil back into his pocket. "Then let's go."

***

Thirty minutes later

I thank Lesley for coming to help and hug her good-bye as we enter the building. She's going back to campus while I'll stay here to support my mom. She really needs me right now so she won't relapse into her old behavior. I don't want him ever to get a grasp on her again.

The officer brings us to his office, at which point he stops us. "I'm sorry, but I need to talk to your mother alone."

I frown and glance at my mother who shrugs. "Everything will be fine, honey."

I sigh and nod. "Okay."

"There's a waiting room right up ahead. You can take a seat in there," the police officer tells me, and I smile and then hug my mother.

With sweaty palms, I make my way to the waiting area

and sit down. I stare anxiously at the watercooler and the bubbles that rise up to the surface every other second. After a while, a man comes out of another room, rubbing his wrists while he's escorted down the hall by a police officer. When he turns his head to me, I gasp.

"Thomas?"

A half-smile appears on his face as he looks at me over his shoulder. "Uh ... hi?"

"What are you doing here?" I ask.

"This way please," the officer interjects, and Thomas follows him. "Be right with you. Don't leave," he says.

I roll my eyes and tap my feet on the floor as I wait. It's not like I can go anywhere without my mom. So I watch Thomas as he fills out a form and gives it back to the police officer. Then he smiles reluctantly and asks him, "Can I just go talk to her for a second? I promise it won't take long."

"Go ahead," the man says, and Thomas nods, then turns to me.

Instinctively, I cross my legs as he comes toward me. His eyes running all over me still make me feel like my clothes are being torn off. But then I see the bruises and cuts on his face and worry seeps back in.

"What happened to you?" I ask.

"What? Oh, this?" He points at his face, and I nod. "Got into a fight."

"Really ..." I muse, narrowing my eyes. "With who?"

He smiles. "Mind if I sit down next to you?"

I take a deep breath and cock my head. "Go ahead."

"Thanks." He sits down beside me, placing his elbows on his knees as he leans on them. "Couldn't help myself. When I saw him, I just had to punch him."

"Who?" I ask, my lip tipping up into a smile.

"Your mom's boyfriend."

My lips part, but I have no idea what to say.

"I found his license plate through your Facebook photos. Figured I could probably still find it at the hospital. I was right."

"You went through my photos to find her boyfriend?" I snort. "Are you insane?"

"Maybe." A cheeky smile forms on his face. "Who wouldn't go mad for a girl like you?"

I shake my head and laugh. "Oh, my god ... you did *not* just say that. Can you be any more corny?"

"Well, it made you laugh, didn't it?" He shrugs. "My job is done."

"Is that why you're here? To make me laugh?"

"Nah, they actually arrested me. Lucky me, I wasn't the one to dish out the first punch, and there were witnesses."

"So you made him hit you?" I ask.

He grins. "Pretty much. Glad I got off with just a fine. It was worth it, though." He rubs his sore chin.

"Why?"

"I just wanted the bastard to pay for what he did to you and your mom," he says. "Simple as that."

"So you didn't do it as a way to try and get me back?"

He cocks his head and makes a face. "Nooo ... Why would I do that? Pfft." He laughs it off and makes a weird gesture with his hand, which makes me chuckle. I try to hide it behind my hand, but he notices anyway.

"But now that I'm here ..." He glances my way and then sighs. "I know you don't want to talk to me, and you don't have to. I just wanted to tell you that I do care. I care a lot about you. So much that I didn't even realize it until it was too late."

I lick my lips, preventing myself from interrupting him because I think I wanna hear this, even though my brain is telling me to stop him. I've already been hurt enough.

"I know what you're thinking. That I'm a piece of shit for stringing you along."

"Are you? Are you stringing me along? Because it sure felt like it."

"I was, but not for the reasons you think ..." He swallows and looks at the floor. "For a long time, I tried to deny the feelings I had for you, thought I'd only bring out the worst in the both of us. And eventually, I did ... because you hate me now."

"Tell me the truth, Thomas. That woman I saw, the one who's been driving you around, who's been talking to you behind my back, who's been to your apartment, probably many times, and even said you two were 'over' ... She's your girlfriend, isn't she?"

"Girlfriend?" He cocks his head and a smile slowly creeps onto his face. "No."

I grimace. "Your wife?"

"No ... She's my sister-in-law."

My brows furrow and my jaw drops. I don't get this at all.

"Actually, more like my ex-sister-in-law." He looks away. "The point is, no, we're not dating, and I'm not seeing her behind your back."

"But ... she ..." I mutter. "Ex ... Sister-in-law." The realization hits me like a brick. "You were married."

Chapter 27

THOMAS

"Exactly. *Were*. Past tense," I say.
"What happened? Did you divorce?" she asks.
"No." I lick my lips. "A few years ago, she died."

***

Two years ago

My heart is racing as I see the scene in front of me unfold.

My wife with tears in her eyes, standing in front of the ten-story building window. Our window. In our home. With a knife in her hand.

I plead with her not to do anything she'll regret.

Thoughts about what I could've done differently spin through my head. Why she keeps going back to this point. This unhappiness. It's always looming in the background, waiting for a chance to spring back up.

Like now.

She's tired of life.

It's been so long since I've last seen a genuine smile that I don't even know what happiness is anymore. At least, not when I look at her.

The confident, cheerful woman I once knew shriveled up and died in front of me. But why?

What drives a person to sit on the edge of a ledge and look out upon their death?

Is it the need to go beyond what we can see in life?

Is what she has not enough?

Every time this happens, it's always something different.

A new house. A new job. This time, it's a baby.

Or rather, the lack of.

We've had the discussion so many times that I started avoiding talking about it altogether. Maybe I shouldn't have turned off that switch. Maybe I should've kept talking. Or maybe I never should have brought it up in the first place.

Because it was me.

Me, who first asked … do you want a baby?

Me, out of all people.

Can you imagine?

I can't.

It's not in my nature, and I'll never be a good father figure. But I wanted to do it for her because I saw that joy in her eyes whenever she saw her friends' babies. Whenever she cuddled them. I could feel it in my heart that this is what she needed.

For a moment in my life, I thought I could fix things.

Fix her.

With a baby.

As if a baby could ever fix anything.

As if it would magically solve all our problems.

It was messed up. And I know now that this is ultimately what led to her sitting on the edge of our window this very second.

Because that baby was a seed that I planted in her head. A seed that would never come to fruition.

Why? Because her body wasn't able to. That's what the doctor said.

For months and months, we tried, and when we got tested, that's what came out.

It wasn't me. God, I begged it was me. I fucking begged that it was me, so she could move on, find another man, and have a baby. So she'd finally be happy.

But that was impossible.

And now, we've ended up here.

Again.

First, it was the scissors.

Then, it was the tub.

Now, it's the window.

Every time, it's something new. Something else she'll try to take away her pain.

How many more times can I save her? How many more times will she allow me to?

When I step closer, she says, "Don't."

I wonder if this is the last time I'll ever see her face

again. If it's the last time I'll hear her voice. It goes through my mind every time she does this, and each attempt is another crack in my heart.

"Please ... come here. We can talk about it."

"No ... we've talked enough. I don't want to do this anymore."

"We can work things out," I say.

"We can't. Nothing can fix this." She points at her belly. "Nothing that can fix *us*."

I don't know why it became this way. Why we became so disconnected. Why we became two people just living together instead of one love.

I swallow and hold up my hand to make her stop, even though I don't dare to step closer, afraid of what she'll do. "Just give me the knife, and I promise I will do something. We can go into therapy again."

"We already did that. It's not working. None of it is." Tears stream down her face. "I'm tired. Tired of this. Tired of life."

"Please don't say that. I need you. This world needs you."

"No," she says, vehemently shaking her head. "You don't. You need a woman who can give you something more. Someone who loves herself."

"But I love you. Isn't that enough?"

"No!" she yells, throwing the knife on the floor. "You don't love me. You don't love me anymore ..."

"Of course, I do," I say, the desperation in my voice seeping through.

She crawls closer to the window and looks over the edge at the ground below. "I don't believe it."

Has she gone this far?

Is her view of this world, of me, so distorted that she can't even see what's right in front of her?

"I don't want a baby. I want you," I say.

"I can't give you what you want, Thomas. Enough is enough. I don't want this pain anymore. I need it to end." She sniffs and smiles softly, but it's faked. "I love you, I always will."

Time seems to stand still as the woman I love turns her head away from me and throws herself out the window.

I scream. Louder than I ever have.

Its hollowness will never reach her in time.

***

Now

"Oh, my god …" Hailey murmurs as I tell my story. "I don't know what to say."

"I don't know what to say either except for the fact that I don't talk about this easily."

She swallows. "I'm sorry. About your wife … and that you have to tell me like this."

I smile at her. "It's okay. I guess it had to come out sooner or later. This time, it was too late. I should've told you sooner, considering what happened."

I rub my hands together and touch my finger where my ring used to be. I threw it in the casket when I buried her, but the mark is still on my finger.

"I was married. And then, I suddenly wasn't. And it broke me. It broke me into a million pieces, which I slowly glued back together over time, but they never became whole again. And now you know why I never tried to get past the flirting phase ever again."

"That's why you were … pushing me away," she says tentatively.

"Yes. I kept ignoring my growing feelings, thinking they were wrong. I kept pushing away the fact that my wife died. But now, I realize that wasn't the right way to deal with it at all." I sigh. "After all, I'm still here, alive, breathing. She'd want me to move on."

She smiles gently. "She'd want you to find someone to love again."

"Exactly," I say, nodding. "And I found it in you."

***

Hailey

I rub my lips together to try to understand, but it's coming slowly.

He didn't want to commit because he was afraid he'd hurt me. Because he was afraid to lose me too.

He chuckles and shakes his head. "It's sad, I know. Pathetic, how I handled life after what happened to her."

"No," I say, grabbing his hand. "I get it now. It's not pathetic."

"Really? When I made the one girl I truly cared about think I was cheating on her? Yeah, that's pathetic."

"But you weren't …" I say. "I just saw you two

together."

"And you put two and two together," he continues. "I know." He looks me deeply in the eye. "But I promise you, Natalie and I are not fucking. Just thinking about it makes my skin crawl. I wouldn't even touch her with a ten-foot pole." He shakes it off. "Like I'd ever want to date my sister-in-law. Nope. Not sexy. She's also my boss, so that would only make it more awkward. Well, ex-boss."

"What?" I stammer . "Your boss? You mean to say she hired you to teach us?"

"Yup. Look, I know it doesn't make a lot of sense, but you have to believe me. This is the truth. She's a friend. Albeit, one I didn't want." He chuckles. "When my wife died, everyone around me blamed me for her suicide, except Natalie. But she was mad … understandably. And even though part of her hated me for what had happened to her sister, she still tried to help me. Got me a job here at the college so I could move on. I got an apartment and tried to move past what happened. I drowned myself in work … and with alcohol and women. I was in a shitty place."

I swallow away the lump in my throat when I hear him say that.

"Well, you know the rest." He clears his throat. "Anyway, she only drove me to school that one time you saw her because my car was at the garage. And that time she wanted to talk to me was because I was messing up again. I have a history, you see …"

"Of what? Chasing school girls?"

"No … just, drinking … and maybe a lot of random sex." He sniffs. "The point is, she was looking out for me. Granted, it was mostly done through scolding."

"Why would she do that?"

"Because she didn't want you to get hurt." He looks up at me. "And because I'm not supposed to hook up with students." He clears his throat. "When she found out about you, she fired me."

"Fired … you got fired?" I don't know why, but I suddenly feel bad. Guilty. I knew it was gonna happen, but still, it's tough to hear.

He shrugs. "Yeah, but I don't really care. Besides, it's not like she could keep me on after finding out. I understand." He smiles at me again. "It was worth it, though. I got to have you in my life, even if it was only for a little while."

He gets up and stares ahead. "You know, I once thought I was unlovable. That I should stay away from everyone because I could only hurt them. I didn't want a relationship because I'd always end up hurting the people that I love. Turns out I was right."

When he tries to walk away, I grab his hand.

He stops and glances at me over his shoulder. "I hurt you, Hailey. I know that. I wish I could turn back time, but I can't. I made the wrong decisions. I put more value in keeping my job than keeping you, and it cost me both. I won't make that mistake again."

I nod and rub my lips together. "I never wanted to lose you," I say. "But when I saw you with her, I thought … I thought …"

"That I was a cheating bastard." He raises a brow. "Yeah, I know. And I had it coming. I should've told you about her before." He cracks his knuckles. "But talking about my past is difficult for me. It makes me feel weak, and

I don't like feeling weak."

He leans in and caresses my cheek, then tips up my chin. "*You* also made me weak."

My brows furrow, but when I try to speak, he places a finger on my lips.

"Weak from your love."

Love.

That word.

It's all I wanted to hear but never got from him.

He pulls me up from my seat with just the tip of his finger. "I know it's too late to say this, as I've already ruined my chance, but I just wanted to say it to make you feel good again because you deserve it. Because it's the truth. I love you, Hailey Walters. And there's nothing you can do about it."

I freeze as he leans in and presses a delicate kiss on my cheeks, smiling after. He turns around and starts to walk away. I want to call out for him to stop, but then a door opens, and my mom steps out. I'm torn, but I know I can't go after him and leave my mother here.

So I stay, staring at him as he opens the door, goes down the steps, and disappears from my view.

Blinking a tear away, I gaze at my mom and ask, "And? How did it go?"

She smiles, tears welling up in her eyes. "They're going to press charges, and I'm hoping he's going behind bars for a long time."

"Really?"

She nods, and I rush to her, hugging her gently as I don't want to hurt her. Finally, justice has been served.

"I'm sorry for all those years ..." she mutters, but I

shush her.

"It's okay, Mom. It's finally over now." I brush the tears from her face and peck her on the cheek. "Let's go home, okay?"

She nods as I grab her hand and walk out the door with my mother by my side.

With the sun shining brightly, I breathe a sigh of relief and stare up at the sky.

Each second we spend on this earth is another one we should cherish. I know that now.

We shouldn't get stuck in a place we don't wanna be, or do things that go against our hopes and dreams. We should chase the things we love, and more importantly, never, ever look back.

My life is falling into place at last. And I know exactly what I wanna do.

Chapter 28

Hailey

A few days later

"Are you sure about this? If you leave, there's no going back," Lesley says as she watches me pack.

"Yes," I say. "I've already filled out the forms. There is no going back."

"What about your mom? Is she okay with it?"

"Yeah ... now that my mom's boyfriend is finally behind bars, she's free to bug me with questions instead." I chuckle. "But she says she's happy as long as I am."

She smiles, but it's followed by a sigh. "Well, I'm sure she's proud of you, and so am I." She hugs me awkwardly from behind, making me laugh.

"Thanks," I say. "But it's really just because I suck at studying."

"True, but you could've fixed your grades easily," she says. "There was still time."

"I don't want more time here," I say. "I want more time out there in the real world. This place isn't for me. I'm not cut out for this—I know that now."

"It's a bit of a waste of all those months you already did finish, though," she says, fetching my clothes from the drawers for me and placing them on the bed next to my suitcase.

"All the more reason to quit now."

"What are you gonna do next?" she asks.

"I don't know …" I say, smiling. "Maybe I'll get a job somewhere in an ice-cream shop."

She grins. "They'd lose money over you because you'd be stuffing your face all the time."

"Shhh!" I nudge her with my elbow. "Don't ruin the plan."

"You could always start up your own business, you know?" she muses. "You'd be able to eat all the ice cream you wanted."

"Hmm …" I mull it over a bit. "That's not even a bad idea."

"What? Nah …"

"Yeah. Why not?" I shrug.

She laughs. "I didn't really peg you as the type to go boss people around."

"No, but I know just the guy for it …"

Her jaw drops. "*Him?*"

"You never know?" I wink.

"Oooh ... so that's why you're quitting college."

I frown and drop my panties in the suitcase. "No, of course not."

"But he was fired too because he was seeing you," she says. "He doesn't blame you for that?"

"No, he blames himself more than anything, actually."

"Strange."

"He and I just ... talked it over."

"And?"

I think about it for a second. "I think we can finally move on. It's good."

"Hmm ... well, as long as you're happy. That's all that matters."

"I am." I look her way. "I mean it, I really am. And it's been a long time since I was last able to say that."

"Yeah ... when was it? Oh yeah, last time I saw you with that dildo." She snorts, and I give her another shove with my elbow. "Speaking of ... you almost forgot it." She holds it out to me.

"Where'd you get that? I was lookin' for it." I snatch it from her hand.

"Under your bed. Where you always put it." She raises her brow. "You're gonna need it now that he's ... gone?"

I grin. "I'll see about that, but it's none of your business."

She laughs. "Good. Keep it that way. I really *don't* wanna know what my best friend and former teacher are doing. Yuck." She sticks out her tongue.

"But you'll come visit me, right? Even if he could be there?"

"Of course," she says, putting her hands against her side. "Like you could survive without me."

I laugh. "True."

"That's nothin' but da tru tru."

I make a face and snort from her reference to a movie we once watched. I think it was *Cloud Atlas*. Not that it matters.

"Wait, aren't you forgetting something?" Lesley holds up a packet of cigarettes.

For a moment, I'm tempted to grab them, but then I don't. "Nah, keep them."

"You sure?" She frowns. "You're quitting?"

"Yeah, I think so." I shrug it off and grab my suitcase, waltzing to the door.

"So ... I'll see you around then?" she says, folding her arms.

I turn around and drop my suitcase, opening my arms. "C'mere, bitch."

She runs into my arms and hugs me, and I slap her on the ass, laughing hard. "Make the boys go crazy for you, but be careful, okay? I'm not gonna have your back anymore, so you gotta have your own."

"Oh, I've had enough parties to last a lifetime now. I'm just gonna settle for studying for a while," she muses, winking as we stop hugging.

"Good. And I don't wanna see you away from this campus unless it's to visit me. You have to succeed."

"Of course. Someone's gotta set the right example," she jokes, and I roll my eyes.

"Right, Les ... bye!" I grab my suitcase and turn around.

She slaps my ass so hard it makes me jolt. "Go get 'em,

bitch."

"Yeah, yeah! You'll be hearing from me. Don't worry. My name will be everywhere, just you wait."

"Good, I'll check the newspaper every day."

"You'd better," I shout as I walk through the hallway.

"See ya!" she yells.

"Love ya!"

And as I take my final glance, I can't help but brush my cheeks. Fucking stray tears messing with my epic escape from college.

But I'm gonna miss that girl ... no doubt about it.

All the more reason to see her soon. And from the sound of her shouting, she'll be checking up on me every day of the week, so I don't think we'll be separated for long.

***

I've been staying at my mom's house for a few days, at least, until I find my own place. She doesn't mind because now she gets to squash me with love every five minutes. Plus, I'm paying rent now that I've finally gotten a proper job.

Well, 'job' ... I'm washing glasses and cleaning floors after closing time for a club near the campus. It's not ideal, but it pays nice, and this way, I get to build up some experience in the field I wanna work in. It's also very close to Lesley, which she finds very convenient. She keeps face-planting the window in the middle of the night to scare the living crap out of me, and it works every single damn time.

Damn her.

Not that I mind.

I kinda like this newfound freedom. Going out into the world. Not giving a shit what anyone thinks. Just living my life.

That, and lounging on the couch while scrolling through my Facebook timeline to see what everyone is up to, like I'm doing now. It's nice to watch them do what they love. And to finally feel like I'm where I'm supposed to be too.

Suddenly, my phone buzzes and a message pops up from a familiar guy.

Thomas: How's the free life going?

Hailey: Good, very good, actually. How did you know?

Thomas: I asked Lesley when you weren't at your dorm room.

Hailey: Stalker. :P

Thomas: I never give up.

Hailey: I know you don't.

Thomas: Unless you want me to, of course.

I pause and think about it for a second, but all I can do is grin like a teenage girl.

Hailey: Don't ever stop.

Thomas: Oh, I won't. I'll be here, lurking in the

shadows, waiting until you're ready. I know you needed a break. I'll wait. I'll wait as long as I have to, even if it's forever.

I suck on my bottom lip and smile.

Hailey: Creeper. :P

Thomas: Sorry. I can get a bit overenthusiastic when it comes to the things I want to keep.

Hailey: Keep? As if you ever had me.

Thomas: N̶o̶t̶ yet … but I will. Someday. And you know, I think that day's coming pretty soon.

Hailey: Oh, really? When?

Thomas: How about Saturday at eight? You know where.

Hailey: Hmm … You mean that place you said you'd never visit again?

Thomas: Just like that mistake I'd never make again.

Hailey: You sure do like things wrong, don't you?

Thomas: Shaken, not stirred. You?

Hailey: We'll see …

Thomas: Yes, we will.

God, he's such an arrogant prick.
But I love him for it.
I can honestly say I do.
Well, not in a get-a-fucking-ring-and-stand-in-front-of-the-altar way, but just the part where I'd say I could give it a shot.

Thomas: You know I'll wait forever. Even if you don't show up. I'll be there the next Saturday too. And the one after that. I'm an eternal party animal. #PartyHard

Hailey: As long as the party is for two.

Thomas: I don't share. You know that.

Hailey: I don't either.

Thomas: So fiery. ... I like that. Just like your hair color.

Hailey: Maybe I'll dye it blue.

It takes him a while to respond.

Thomas: Blue ... almost the hottest part of a flame. #Chemistry

Hailey: You really don't give up, do you?

Thomas: Not when it comes to you. And you know why? Because the more time I spend away from you, the more I realize that I don't want to be anywhere other than right next to you. In whatever way possible. Because nothing's going to change the fact that I'm madly in love with you, Hailey Walters. So ... would you go out on a *real* date with me?

I'm smiling from ear to ear.

Hailey: I thought you'd never ask ...

Epilogue

THOMAS

As I walk through the club, I know exactly where to go. It's familiar ground, and this isn't my first rodeo.

But it may be my last.

When I spot her across the room, my heart practically bounces out of my chest. Crazy, huh? How within a few weeks, a man can go from his dick bursting out of his pants to this. A weak pile of mush at the sight of her.

She's just as beautiful as ever with her red bob, which now fades to blue at the bottom. But her physical appearance isn't what attracts me the most. It's her spirit. Her will to live and to defy everything and everyone around her.

All this time, I was searching for something—something

to make me feel alive—and I found it in her. I was so afraid to love because I'd only known a love that was slipping away. But Hailey ... she's wanted me since the day I met her. Never once did she give up. She was never afraid to love, even when she'd felt it so little from others.

I'm no longer afraid. I'm no longer stumbling in and out of her arms.

She was mine from the beginning.

We weren't falling.

We were running to each other.

Just as we are now.

With a smug smile, I approach her as she picks up her drink and takes a sip, casually eyeing my body from top to bottom and back. When our eyes lock, she puts her drink down on the table and smiles cheekily.

"Hey," I say. "Used your fake ID, I see."

"Hi." She giggles, a blush appearing on her cheeks. "It still comes in useful."

"How are you? Been up to something good since leaving college?"

"Yeah ... just work and stuff. Not much else."

I narrow my eyes. "So that whole business thing you were talking about?"

"Not yet," she says, chuckling. "But I'll get there, eventually. And you?"

"Same," I say. "Still looking for that perfect job."

"Ahh ... look, I'm sorry about—"

"Don't be," I interrupt. "We both lost something. And maybe gained something new ..." The left side of my lip tips up into a smile.

"Hmm ... true. I never thanked you for doing what you

did."

"What?"

"With my mom's boyfriend and all …" She shrugs.

I shake my head. "Don't mention it. Really. That asshole deserved what he had coming. And besides, I needed to make things right."

She smiles. "I know. I just wanted to thank you."

It grows quiet again, but then she asks, "I hope it's not keeping you up at night."

"What? That I put a man in jail?"

"Yeah."

"Nope. Not even one bit."

"And your other nightmares?"

My forehead creases for a second, but then I relax. "Haven't had them in a while."

"Really? Well, at least you got that going for ya …"

I place a hand on her arm. "It's because of you that I no longer have them."

Her brows furrow. "What do you mean?"

"Other dreams have replaced the nightmares," I whisper. "And by other dreams, I mean filthy ones about a certain bad student …" I wriggle my eyebrows, making her roll her eyes and playfully slap me.

"Oh, stop," she says, chuckling.

I shrug it off. "It's the truth."

"Well, I'm happy for you, even if I feel a little creeped out. It's just damn shitty you had to lose your job over me."

"No, it's not your fault," I say.

Her face scrunches up, like she's thinking about something all of the sudden. "You know, maybe we could start up that business together. Then we'd both be doing something worthwhile."

I frown but then think about it … "That's not even a bad idea."

"Oh." She laughs. "It was just a random thought."

"No, I like it." I smile, and she smiles back, but then our conversation grows quiet again.

"Awkward," she muses.

"It doesn't have to be." I grin and hold out my hand. "Want to dance?"

Her brows lift and she grabs my hand, so I gently tug her along to the dance floor. I place my hand on her waist and put hers on my shoulder as we start to dance to the music.

"It feels so strange to be here again with you," she says.

"Strange good, or strange bad?"

"Both." She lifts her shoulders, smiling devilishly.

"So let's just start again." I pull her close. "Let's pretend we're strangers."

"Strangers?" She snorts. "Right."

"Yeah. Do I know you? Because I would love to."

She laughs, and it's the most delightful thing I've heard in a long time. "All right, mister."

"Oh, I like it when you call me that." I swoop her off her feet and twirl her around. "But my name is Thomas. Thomas Hard. Pleasure to meet you."

She rolls her eyes when I raise my brow at her. "Fine, my name is Hailey Walters, but you knew that already."

"And I'll want to know it every damn day of the week," I murmur, whisking her close. "Tell me, Miss, do you like to play games?"

"Depends on what kind of game," she whispers.

"Dangerous games. Except this time ... I'm not your teacher, and you're not my student. And we can do whatever we want ... whenever we want. Exactly the way we want it."

"Does that mean I have a say in things too?" she jests.

"Depends on the situation." I grab her ass and squeeze. "Because you should know something about me, and that's the fact that I like dishing out orders to naughty girls."

"Ooh ..." She sucks in a breath as my tongue dips out to lick her neck.

"Are you a naughty girl?" I ask.

"Depends ... are you the right guy?" She moans as I end my lick with a kiss.

"I can be anyone you want me to be ... as long as I can be the one for you."

"Yes," she murmurs. "Fuck, yes."

I grin against her skin. "Is that a yes to just one night, or for the rest of your life?"

"Maybe ... Does that mean I'm more to you than just a girl you can fuck?" She bites her lip, and it makes me want to lean in and bite it for her.

"I think the words 'I love you' already made that quite clear, didn't they?" I say.

"Say it again," she whispers.

"I love you, Hailey."

I grab her face with both hands and smash my lips to hers, not giving a shit whether anyone's watching, if anyone knows us, or where we are.

I want her to be mine.

And I don't give a damn that it cost me my job or my reputation.

She is worth it.

When our lips detach, I want nothing more than to kiss her again, but my desire to be alone with her takes over. "Come home with me. Not as a girl I can fuck but as my girlfriend. The one I want to be with outside the bedroom too."

"Depends… Do you think Ninja will be jealous of you?"

I laugh. "Maybe we should get another cat … to keep him company."

She grins. "A pussy named ice cream."

"Ice cream?"

"Yeah … so I can buy her a matching collar for my earrings. Plus, what cat doesn't wanna lick some ice cream?" she jokes, making me laugh.

"Perfect. So you ready to go home then?"

"Fuck, yeah," she says, chuckling as I nibble her earlobe.

"Hmm … Then let's get out of here. But first, I want to make a stop at your mom's house."

She frowns and her lips part as she opens her eyes again, dazed from my kiss. "What? Why?"

I lick my lips and try to bite away the smile on my face, but it's not effective. "Because we're going to pick up that pink dildo you were talking about. Mr. Rabbit?"

Her eyes widen and then she bursts out into laughter. "Oh, god. You mean Mr. Pink?"

"Mr. Pink? It has a name?" When I laugh, she playfully punches me.

"Shut up, like you never gave your dick a name."

"At least my dick's attached to my body," I say.

"Like that makes it any different. Pfft."

A grin spreads across my face. "No matter, that only

makes it better."

"What? You wanna use my dildo?"

"I told you it would happen. It was only a matter of time. I want to do loads of stuff with you, including but not limited to shoving my—"

"Okay, okay, I get it. Geez, you sound like a lawyer."

"I just know what I want, and I'm not afraid to show it," I muse. "And it was only a matter of time before we ended up back here."

"Back together?"

"I was going to say 'back in this club,' but yeah, that'll do."

She shakes her head and rolls her eyes, which I think is so cute, I can't help but kiss her again while she's doing it. And that's just it.

All I want to do is kiss her, and I don't ever want to stop.

Life's a string of random moments, moments you can either push away or enjoy for what they are. And now, I've finally learned to enjoy this moment just the way it is.

THANK YOU FOR READING!

Thank you so much for reading Bad Teacher. I hope you enjoyed the story!

For updates about upcoming books, please visit my website, www.clarissawild.blogspot.com or sign up for my newsletter here: www.bit.ly/clarissanewsletter.

I'd love to talk to you! You can find me on Facebook: www.facebook.com/ClarissaWildAuthor, make sure to click LIKE. You can also join the Fan Club: www.facebook.com/groups/FanClubClarissaWild/ and talk with other readers!

Enjoyed this book? You could really help out by leaving a review on Amazon and Goodreads. Thank you!

ALSO BY CLARISSA WILD

Dark Romance
Delirious Series
Killer & Stalker
Mr. X
Twenty-One
Ultimate Sin
VIKTOR

New Adult Romance
Fierce Series
Blissful Series

Erotic Romance
The Billionaire's Bet Series
Enflamed Series

Visit Clarissa Wild's website for current titles.
http://clarissawild.blogspot.com

ABOUT THE AUTHOR

Clarissa Wild is a New York Times & USA Today Bestselling author, best known for the dark Romance novel Mr. X. Her novels include the Fierce Series, the Delirious Series, Stalker, Twenty-One (21), Ultimate Sin, Viktor, and Bad Teacher. She is also a writer of erotic romance such as the Blissful Series, The Billionaire's Bet series, and the Enflamed Series. She is an avid reader and writer of sexy stories about hot men and feisty women. Her other loves include her furry cat friend and learning about different cultures. In her free time she enjoys watching all sorts of movies, reading tons of books and cooking her favorite meals.

Want to be informed of new releases and special offers? Sign up for Clarissa Wild's newsletter on her website clarissawild.blogspot.com.

Visit Clarissa Wild on Amazon for current titles.

Printed in Dunstable, United Kingdom